D0049279

HANNAH VERSUS THE TREE

HANNAH VERSUS THE TREE

LELAND DE LA DURANTAYE

McSWEENEY'S
SAN FRANCISCO

McSWEENEY'S
SAN FRANCISCO

Jacket design by Sunra Thompson

McSweeney's and colophon are registered trademarks of McSweeney's, an independent publisher based in San Francisco. McSweeney's exists to champion ambitious and inspired new writing, and to challenge conventional expectations about where it's found, how it looks, and who participates. McSweeney's is a fiscally sponsored project of SOMArts, a nonprofit arts incubator in San Francisco.

Printed in the United States.

ISBN 978-1-944211-50-9

10 9 8 7 6 5 4 3 2 1

www.mcsweeneys.net

For her

Did you really think she wouldn't come for you, in the night, like you came for so many, during so many nights? Had you really thought they were all just rumors, rumors about what she was and what she could do? It appears that you did. Just as it appears that you no longer do. I am, as your lawyers suggest, perhaps no more than a spoiled, petulant child who knows so little of the world that it is breathtaking. On the other hand you are an old woman who lives so far removed from the world, separated by firewalls of wealth, as to live apart from it. Who is to say which of us understands less? Except about the matter at hand. Thus your offer.

In exchange for the dropping of all charges against all parties, even Annika, I will give you what you ask. But know that it will not be what you want. For it cannot help. It cannot better your situation, cannot slow, let alone halt, what's coming. It would indeed be difficult to imagine worse press than you are currently getting. Unless, that is, the world were to see the real reason for your fall. Then it would get worse. Much.

In telling the story of now no future chronicler will fail to note this as the end of the long influence of the House of Syrl. It is rare for a family to live so long, through so many generations, so much cold water and chainmail and so many ships and wars, fracturing and healing, fusing and dividing, always resilient, until now. A family of such descent is a rare thing. Not one in a million knows it. So it will be noted. But the why is another matter. Will they know why, will they know how Hannah Silke Sylva Syrl brought down her entire fearsome ancient house around her, like Samson, except that she was a girl, and could see, and did it with her mind? That will be up to you.

I assume that you know little of the facts of my family in any but the most distorted manner, thanks to the accounts of your nephews, who are, as you may know, psychopaths. The answer to your lawyers' first question is that Hannah was six. I was six. She was walking across woodchips with your daughter-in-law. You may say what you like about my mother, and I have gathered that you do, but not that she lacked initiative. My mother approached your daughter-in-law, whom I had assumed to be a duchess or a sorceress or an astrophysicist or in some other way deeply inaccessible, coming from so far away as they did, and it was arranged. After a few hours of erranding to one place and another, all boring, the dogs impatient, we at last came to a stop in front of a glass house. As we walked towards it I could see into it, its green, its tree, Hannah.

It smelled nice inside your son's home. I had never been in a house with a tree growing through it before. We descended a level and sat down next to a fireplace, all warm wood and the colors of children, red, orange, yellow, and were silent. I had a hat and it was pulled low and no, I did not wish to take it off. Looking directly at Hannah at that range seemed as safe as staring at the sun, endless heat and light and source of all life. I recall everything in the room provided it was within a few feet of the ground. I remember a sculpture of Sedna, its soapstone smooth and fluid, and how I moved over it in my mind again and again, looking for calm. When my silence was noted I asked what it was, this woman becoming something else, or so many other things. Hannah began to answer that she was a princess in the northernmost north when your daughter-in-law said in a loud voice that it was an Inuit mermaid, giving Hannah a nudge, for it was not, as Hannah later told me, a story for guests. Or children.

The mothers left and Hannah approached. I saw bare honey-colored feet, each big toe with a daub of nail polish, one red, one orange. With the tips of her fingers Hannah slowly lifted the brim of my hat until, at last, I saw. Her eyes were blue, like the sea and flecked with bits of gold, like sunken treasure. The way she spoke was festive, as was the whole cadence of her playful little person. She was to show me the house.

I followed her down a glass corridor, the green of Michigan on all sides, as she told me the story of Sedna. Many of the objects she presented were strange. Those that looked like the water, such as Sedna, were Inuit, Hannah said. Seal, narwhal, killer whale, kayak, shaman. They are my mother's things, she said. But the majority of things in the house were another kind of foreign, from another world, from the South, from Hannah's youth, from Ecuador. We went there to stop my father's family from digging a hole in the Amazon, she said. And so it was that I first heard of what you do. Or did.

As Hannah told me the dangers of the jungle I remember the sky grew bluer until it couldn't anymore and then turned darker and the insects streamed from the forest behind the house, enlivening the air, bringing birds and bats. What do you think they think of one another? Hannah asked. Do the birds think the bats are good flyers, but change their minds all the time? That they have great technical skill but no real program? Or do they know that the bats are screaming their way through the dark? And the bats, Hannah asked, what do they think? Maybe they don't care, she said with a little sigh. Then she turned to me, gold glimmering in depths, and dared me to soap-opera kiss her.

The answer to the second question on your lawyers' list is that I met your son the following day. We were to go to the lake with my mother and him as expedition leaders. When he pulled up in front of our house your son was wearing large maple-leaf sunglasses, each eye a red leaf against white, which he removed to greet my mother. I remember asking him how he could see through them and liking him right away. Hannah said that the glasses were hers and that being Canadian was something to take seriously. During the drive we played fingers in the backseat and discussed the depth of the ocean. When we arrived and were released we raced down the sand to the water and I remember the hot and the shock of cold and Hannah surfacing, the sea in her eyes, the sun on her freckles, and that she had a new dare.

There was an accidental crayfish death. I remember how Hannah knelt down, her hair dripping, so different after the water, so dark, checking to see if it was pretending. When she saw that it wasn't, she murmured something she would murmur many times before I understood it. Whenever your grand-daughter saw a thing die, she always said, softly, a single word, one she wouldn't repeat. One of the Ecuadorians had taught her to do this, an old woman who would sit with Hannah and who told her that life is really just energy and energy never does anything but move, but that every time the flow of energy returns, every time there is death, you should watch it return. That's piety. That is real reincarnation, the old woman said. Not as the same mind, not as the same person, not so selfish as that. Just returning to the earth. And so to the crayfish, as later to a wasp, a frog, a rabbit, a lobster, a deer, a dog, a horse, a possum, Hannah whispered, softly, *return*.

Meanwhile, something else was happening. As we made things out of sand and ran and swam and dove and performed rituals, farther up the beach, amid the bright tumult of umbrellas, your son and my mother began something else. They began the Divide.

In my home Hannah and I were often left to the care of my mother's dog, a bearish Akita named Alaska who protected us with an intensity that was alarming to strangers and soothing to us. And so it was that we were the first to see her inscrutable face take on a new inscrutable expression, the first to see her belly grow heavy. We watched it as it grew and grew, every week heavier, more unbelievable, and one evening while my parents were having a party for people from California she went deep into the garden behind the densest shrubs and dug a hole. The adults were celebrating something, maybe the solstice. There was a bonfire. Your son and daughter-in-law were there. My sister Gaby found us on the roof of the garage and told us where Alaska was and why she was there and to take her water. Alaska, normally so quiet, made the sounds of her ancestors, whining, whimpering, groaning, grunting, keening her young into the world, calling them to her. We sat with her as one after another the new creatures emerged wet and strange and warm and, as soon became clear, of different fathers. Some adults approached, big, loud, smelling of alcohol, and as they came close Alaska sprang up and stepping in front of us, in front of her young, she growled so deep and long and low that we felt it in our little bodies and when my father saw Alaska's teeth he sent everyone in the other direction. Only we were allowed close.

The next morning, I awoke to a strange sound and found Hannah outside, her cheeks red, her feet wet from the dew, her hand full of the chestnuts she had been lobbing through my window. You sleep too late, she said. Let's go see what they're doing. The puppies were sleepwalking around their little world, nestling against the body of their mother, tumbling over us, over one another, over themselves. Soon their eyes opened the color of quicksilver and it was then clear to all that Alaska had gotten around. Week after week Hannah would throw chestnuts beneath a sky still grey with sleepiness and we would go down and sit with the puppies and listen to the old creaking house wake up around us, the heavy steps of my father, the tripping ones of my mother, my sister hard on her heels. One morning my mother came down and asked what we were doing up so early and Hannah, her freckles bright, her eyes warm, said that we were taking care of the puppies so that Alaska could rest. It's a responsibility, she said.

Before the Divide our world heated up. It was like a return to the very beginning, to the first circle of warmth. From our parents had always come the warmest reason. They had taught us to read and roller-skate and swim and that the world was exciting, dangerous, large, surprising, original. They said that things had causes and what they were, told us what the stars were and what ice was, why the sun set and the earth turned and the weather changed and Alaska didn't talk. They were proud of their ways of presenting the very complex to the very small. Pulsars. Ocean currents. The size of the universe. The age of the planet. The evolution of species. Insider trading. And as they came closer to the Divide they grew even warmer, more and more present, more and more affectionate, forever telling us something, showing us something, reading us something, trying to hold themselves in place through us. But we didn't know that. All we knew was that it was warm. And then one morning we awoke to strange clouds in a strange sky, the colors saturated, the air charged, the storm come. Like all terrible storms it began with things that had always been fixed in place flying through the air. That night, as it continued to rage, I snuck down the stairwell and found my sister there already and what we heard next we could not believe, not even Gaby, who could believe so much. Krakatoa is what Gaby called it. She was learning about volcanoes in school. Don't tell Hannah about Krakatoa, she told me the next morning before school. *Nada Krakatoa, claro?*

Hannah was not in school. I found her behind her house, her back against an oak tree, and before she recognized me her eyes flashed fire. She was wrapped in her father's old peacoat, crying to the forest. She said the coat was from where her father was born, from across the seas, from your place. She said that it was made for more than one generation. To her it smelled like him. To me it smelled like her. Above its collar Hannah's eyes were red and she was pale and as I told her about Krakatoa I saw that she already knew. What followed followed fast. The collapse of civil order in our households was simultaneous and complete. We understood impulsive behavior well enough. We were, after all, children. But we had no sense of what was impelling them, no idea what sex was. We could barely ride bikes. Our history teacher told us that by the end of their reign the Venetians had magnificent hats and robes, serene and flowing, and that when, after ruling the Mediterranean for centuries, they fell apart and sold themselves to Napoleon, who then sold them to Austria, their last doge was seen racing down the palace's hallways taking off his robes, his hat, ribbons, rings, vestments, letting fall the signs of power as he went, so that no one get any ideas about his subsequent responsibility, or availability for comment. It was like that.

Gaby's reaction was the most violent and, from her perspective, the most effective. She flipped out so hard on our parents that they complied with her demand and the next thing I knew she was packing for the boarding school to which her boyfriend had been sent, so far away I needed to be shown it on a map not of the state but the country. She was not often gentle with me, but she was then. Hannah and I were in my room tracing an old map of the Great Lakes and she came in and told us to drop the crayons and listen, that we had nothing to do with it, that it was *exclusively their insanity*, a phrase she made us repeat. Then she wished us luck and was gone.

If you come in from the cold of the north, from the snows of the upper peninsula, nothing but snow and bears and wolves and wind and ice and cold water, and you are in a cabin, before a roaring fire, and you begin to warm yourself, and the numbness starts to give way to tingling and feeling and you drink something warm and the heat returns and you lie by the fire, too warm to move, and fall asleep, and you wake and it is night and now there is no more fire and no more cabin, only huge starry darkness, and it is snowing and you are alone with the bears and the wolves and the cold is final and is coming, ever more of it. It was like that.

I remember footsteps on the staircase, the crunching of gravel, the angry sound of slamming, the roar of the car, the lilac tree scraping its roof, and walking to my mother, so still, so far away, and as I was about to put my arms around her leg she let out a scream as loud as her body could make. I thought there was something coming up from the basement, for what else could make her scream like that, and then my father returned and I heard him say your son's name, again and again, and I didn't understand what they were saying, only that they were hard heavy words made to hurt.

I tried to imagine the protest where my parents had met and went to the back of the garage where the vines hung low and it smelled of firewood and turpentine. Beneath layers of spider web I found the signs. My father was very pro-spider and forbade Gaby and me from killing them, in part because they eat mosquitoes and in part because he thought they had a right to be there, a feeling not shared by the Californians, raised to fear black widows and brown recluses, which kill children. My hands full of webs, I took one of the protest signs and repurposed it. I remember writing different things on the two sides. One of them was NO MORE FIGHTING. I knew that a protest was not a place for a complicated platform. I carried it into the kitchen. After a crushed moment of silence, my parents, the Bright Ones, turned to me, and it was working, like when a gust of wind hits a fire and the flames disappear and for a moment the fire is gone, but it has to return, there is too much heat in the wood, and soon the embers are redder than ever.

I put on my baseball cleats and went out the back door. I remember standing beneath the tree with its little apples that we would try and hit over the house with badminton rackets and I went through the pines and the elms and the maples reaching up into the darkness. Approached from the woods, Hannah's house was confusing. I knocked on a window, afraid I would see your son. I saw Hannah. I remember how wide-eyed she looked at me. She led me to her room with the slow dance of stars on the ceiling and I remember climbing into her bed next with my cleats still on and the warmth of her and the smell of her and the safe of her. I remember crying and her singing me a song in Portuguese. She didn't know what it meant, she said, but was sure it was good.

The answer to the next item on your lawyers' list is that yes, your brother was most certainly involved in your ruin, but not as you suspect. At the Divide two individuals essential to your end entered our lives. In light of our parents' recent behavior we regarded all adults with suspicion, with two exceptions: the Old One and the Wise One. The Wise One you know as well as a sister like you can know a brother like him. The Old One was my great-grandfather and you did not have the pleasure. He was in many senses a super-adult, having lived a terrific number of adult years. And yet Hannah and I wondered whether adulthood was not something you might grow out of, for he thought as we did and so had our trust.

Rules had become for us things to break, to break for the feeling of breaking, so as to tell the powers that be to be differently. In this we found a true ally in the Old One. He lived beyond the rules of my house, beyond the rules of any house, doing and saying all sorts of things, in his limited capacity to do and say things, which were clearly subject to another law, an older one. He was grandfathered into himself, as Gaby said, and did as he pleased.

One day the Old One bent forward towards us, his eyebrows raised, as though in outrage, and said, I am decrepit. But I would be precious if I were a killer whale. It is normal that they do not listen to you, he said. You don't know how things work. But it is not normal that they do not listen to me. Once the old were prized. For many mammals, for elephants, lions, wolves, the old are not just useful, they are essential, although the Old One conceded that aged females were more useful than aged males. The same applied to the people who stopped before this step in civilization, he said, the step from hunter-gatherers to farmers. His age encouraged him to take the long view, Hannah observed. If a tribe loses its elders it is fucked, he said. Fucked. Where do you find water in dry years? Which of the red berries is poisonous? What is the weakness of the tribe over the hill? What do you do when the caribou change their migration route? Where do you find salmon? How do you survive snakebite? When the aged go, the pack, the pod, the family, the tribe loses all that useful fucking information. People think these things are on the internet, he said. People have no idea.

The next day he told us a long, forking story which involved him being somewhere far in the north, alone, in a canoe, gliding along a little creek linking two lakes, and seeing, on the shore, a great bear, drinking or fishing. It reared up, he said, and with all of itself roared at him and he did not just hear it, he felt it, felt it vibrate through him, through the air, through the water, through the canoe, through the paddle. He looked from Hannah's eyes to mine and said, slowly, *That is the real world.*

We didn't think of ourselves as being on a line which, given time, even lots of it, led to him. He was too old for that, his body hardened and thinned and stiffened and worn smooth by extreme age, having grown out of frailty into something else entirely. And it is only those who have begun to age who find the old frightening. To the young they're just exotic. The Old One ate little, slowly, and with annoyance. He seemed to live from the fire of whiskey, which Hannah and I tasted once and were shocked by. A touch to the lips was enough to fill your whole head with fire. And this was the Old One's water, Hannah said in wonder.

The Old One's place in the family was fixed by my father. He had taught my father the names of the trees and how to track animals, taught him the forests and the lakes, the winds and the currents, taught him to canoe, to sail, shoot, start fires, and be an animal among animals. The Old One taught my father all the things he had failed to teach his own son. I don't know them either. They skip generations. In return for making him a man, my father revered the Old One. When his Ancientness, as Gaby called him, asked my father to kill him, with a pillow, in his nursing home, saying it wouldn't be hard, saying he would rather die than live another day with all these dying fucking strangers, my father took him and installed him in our house, like an idol. For nothing in the world would my father have wanted his parents or his siblings or any other member of his family in his house for more than absolutely necessary. But the Old One was different. The Old One was a delight.

The Old One had wintered in the upper peninsula of Michigan as a boy, been around the Great Lakes, moved along the shore of Lake Superior into Canada. He had been to Hudson Bay, above the Arctic Circle. He had been charged by a bear. He had killed moose. He knew a great deal about foxes. He explained to us in detail the guns of his youth. It took time to load them, he said. You had one shot. If you shot at a moose or a bear and did not kill it, he said, it would charge and kill you before you had time to reload. And the killing would be very animal, he said. Now it is all different. Now there are degenerates who shoot them out of helicopters with assault weapons. They would not do that here, he said, staring furiously at an old rifle on the wall. The Old One had killed his own before. In World War I. It was a thing he had been made to do, he said. Never kill anyone, he said to us in a way that was intense, given that we were seven, and interesting, given that one day we would.

Being a lone, small thing in a huge forest, on a giant lake, with all those woods, all that water, all that snow and cold and wind and sun, all those animals, all those days and nights had made the Old One's mind a sharp thing. He was irascible in the extreme. He was particularly abusive concerning Native Americans. Unlike the majority of the people around whom he had been raised, he not only knew natives, he preferred them. He said the French were more trustworthy than the English, Canadians more trustworthy than Americans, Indians more trustworthy than all—except the Iroquois. The Ottawa were far and away the most trustworthy and he told us we could always rely on them. We didn't know how to tell him that they were gone. He said the Chippewa and the Ojibwa could be trusted with care, the Cree with caution, and the Iroquois not at all. As bad as the English, he said, bearing down on us with all his agedness. As bad as the English. Which was bad.

Sometimes the Old One would not speak for days. We would sit with him and watch the water, the sun in the trees, on the lake, wondering what story he was telling himself, what unimaginable things he was remembering. During one such silence my father passed by and told us that when the Old One was born there were no planes, let alone the entire earth ringed with satellites from which stream a constant flow of irrelevant information. So sometimes he just pauses to take it all in. We could go play.

One evening Hannah fought to stay, demanding that she be allowed to stay, defying her father. The Old One was delighted by her resistance, as he was delighted by all resistance, and told me something—while Hannah continued to rage against your son in the backyard—that took time to understand. She's different in the oldest way, he said. You recognize it immediately, even if you've never seen it before. I asked what it was and he said the name did not much matter. I first saw it in an Ottawa woman when I was your age, he said. It's familiar like nothing else. Hannah can do what the Ottawa could do. She looks at a thing you can't hide.

On the appointed day we were called to assembly and formally informed of the terms of the Divide, of the multiplication of homes, of the departure of your son. For months, teachers and neighbors and random strangers and our parents kept trying to explain a thing they didn't understand. All except the Old One. As the Divide deepened the Old One spoke to us not of romantic love or adult responsibility but instead of bears, endless stories about bears and moose and wolves and a coalition of tribes on the west coast of Lake Michigan called the Nation of Fire. With whom you did not fuck, he said. He showed us an old French map of their lands with the notation of a Frenchman saying that they were dangerous and most fiery indeed. The room from which the Old One watched the lake was lined with old maps, the only possessions he had insisted follow him, 16th and 17th century maps of New France and its lakes. He would point to them as he told his sagas, the sun setting into the water in front of him, naming the streams and rivers and lands controlled by the Nation of Fire. Story upon story, the tales of the tribe, and my father heard parts of them as he came and went and would tell us that many were ones that even he had never heard himself. He told my mother that this meant the Old One was dying, for why else would he tell his great-grandson about snow and bears and what it felt like to kill a man.

Once Michigan was just trees. No one spoke English, or French. The people spoke Potawatomi (a name Hannah and I admired). They spoke Huron, Chippewa, Ottawa. Some spoke faraway languages like Sioux, Iroquois, Arapaho. Trees and bears and Potawatomi, bears raking their claws down the trunks of trees, and wolves, and deer and moose and ravens and even the small things, like badgers and wolverines, dangerous, for badgers and wolverines will fight anything, anytime, of any size. Whenever the Old One mentioned them he paused to look at me. When he arrived in our home he had asked what I knew about fighting, fearing the worst from pacifists, fearing that my father had not done his ancestral job. I told him the truth, which was that Gaby had taught me to fight. He said that was insufficient. He said that my father was a good and even a brave man, but not to listen to him about fighting, and still less to my mother. Gaby he left up to me, for the Old One had had an older sister of his own, and the Old One knew Gaby. Bullies take countless forms, he said. The thing that is bullying grows like a weed in the world, it grows everywhere, from fear, and the only thing to do when you are confronted by it is to bend down and rip it right out of the fucking ground. *Exemplary*, he said, you must be *exemplary*. You need word to get around not to fight you, otherwise you'll spend all your time either fighting or getting things taken from you. And having things taken from you is not pleasant. Ask the Iroquois. Even if you lose, make everyone around see that you are a badger, a wolverine, small but ferocious, small but excessive, that you fight with total and exemplary fury at any time over any thing until you lack the strength to stand. And then you still bite.

Gaby told him about my getting beat up by another of his great-grandchildren. How he smiled at my blood when I came in. Your sister says that you fought for a long time even though you had no chance, which is good, he said. But she said you could have fought longer. I asked if Gaby really said that and he said he knew it from the fact that she said I could stand afterwards. Never stop while you can stand. He might win, but if you want him to leave you be he has to remember, he has to feel in his face and his ribs and his swollen hands that every time he wants to push you he will have to fight you, and that it will take a long time and be tiring and painful. The only way to have any peace in this world, and, frankly, I don't think this is made clear enough to you, is that when attacked you are to be a little badger, you are to be a little fucking wolverine.

To Hannah, however, he taught something else. He taught her to be a wolf, and in this way contributed to your fall as much as anyone. The puppies born during the party grew healthy, happy, and different. Half were sired by an amiable lab-ish mutt named Bruce who lived around the lake. But half of the litter was very visibly not his. The father of the other pups had gone unseen, declared husky by default given the ears and the fur and the strange look in their eyes. The others saw and did much more than the pups my mother called the Brucei. They wrestled constantly, in permanent tussle, even the female, even Sedna. The Brucei would take breaks, laying around happily wondering at existence. But not them. They learned how to open the latch on their pen before the Brucei knew there was a pen, let alone a latch. And over them the Old One watched.

When the pups were eleven weeks old he summoned us, had us shut the door, lock it, sit down, be quiet, and said that once he told us what he had to tell us we would be forbidden from speaking about it to anyone ever with no exceptions. He asked if we understood. The cottage we went to in the summer had been built by the Old One's father when no other structure was in sight of it and only an insane person would think of wintering there. To the south there were people, to the north was wild. The Old One told us that he had seen dogs his whole life, dogs of every kind, hunting dogs, hounds, huskies, retrievers, pointers, terriers, sheep dogs and cattle dogs and stray dogs and wild dogs and even Inuit dogs. And he had seen wolves. Having a wolf is illegal, he said, but there are a lot of illegal things people do up here. People here are very hit or miss, he said slowly, very hit or miss. He asked for one of the puppies and Hannah placed Sedna in his lap. With the lake and the night before him the Old One then told us how sled dogs were bred. He said that if you mate a sled dog with a wolf, or a half-wolf, the puppies will be stronger, faster, sharper, better at pulling a sled. But if there is too much wolf they will not obey, and the mushers kill those pups because they know they will never be able to control them. They start selecting when they are as young as her, he said, getting rid of the pups that are too aggressive, too independent, too wolf. You learn to recognize it, he said, for it is very recognizable. Then he lifted in his hands the only female of her kind, his eyes aglitter with ancient interest, and told the bright warm little creature that whoever her father was, he had wolf blood. Lots of it, he said. And then he wished her a long life.

There were two paths, the Old One said. On both you lose something. You can either lose them or a huge portion of your free time. He could tell my father. I don't know what he would do, the Old One said. Your father respects wildness, but he is busy, and he doesn't want trouble with your mother. The Brucei will be easy, he said. They will be happy to serve, happy to obey, easy to find homes for. They will be good dogs. Looking down at Sedna as she chewed his finger he said that she would be something else. Her mother is a dog, a good strong dog who will teach her to be the same. But she will not always think like her mother. Sometimes she will think more dangerously. Like her father. Her will is going to be large and will occupy all the space available to it. When she is strong she will know it. She will want to decide, she will want to hunt, killing will come naturally to her. And if she kills a dog, she dies. If she kills they will catch her and kill her, he said. Some people have no sense for animals, no ear or nose for them. These people are dangerous, for they have no idea they are animals, and it is dangerous not to know you are an animal, if you are an animal. Animals are never aggressive because they lack some moral resolve, he said, never because they are evil. They are aggressive because they want something, aggressive because they are scared of something, and so they send out pulses of aggression, to see your reaction, to see whether you respond calmly, or whether you too become emotional, frightened, aggressive. If you are serene, right in the face and heat of their emotion, she will understand. The Old One cradled Sedna and said that six months from now she will not yet be half her size and yet already will be bigger, faster and stronger than you both by a huge margin. And she will not be alone. A lone wolf changes with the arrival of another member of the pack. They lose it for joy. It's the most moving thing I ever saw in the North, it makes you strong to see, makes you warm to see. Rubbing against one another, ears low, tails moving, noses touching, making little dolphin leaps. They love being together, are strong when they are together, and are dangerous when together. They will respond to an attack on anyone in their circle, including an attack on the Brucei, with one thought and that is kill. It is incredibly hard work. We start in the morning.

We did. And continued every day for a year. I remember holding Hannah's hand at the Old One's funeral, Sedna and Alaska sniffing the earth, tails low. His was our first death, soon followed by your son's. There were a surprising number of people at the Old One's funeral. An Ottawa attended. No Iroquois, as Hannah observed. The Ottawa didn't bend down towards us like other people, he dipped into a squat, strong in it, and he looked carefully at me, at Hannah, and smiled. After my father and his sisters and my mother and Gaby and I had all taken our turns dropping a clump of earth, Hannah walked to the edge, bent low, and as she let hers fall said, softly, *Old One, return.*

As concerns your brother, the Wise One, his involvement began later. When Alexander the Great was a boy his father saw what there was to see, saw that his son was unusual, and so found for him an unusual teacher, the best of Plato's academy in faraway Athens. Alexander's father paid Aristotle's price, which was not particularly high, for Aristotle did not particularly care for money, and the philosopher then came to live with the young prince in a faraway land a night and a day and a night by sea. And in that strange place with its strange plants and odors and food and light, with its strange customs and women and men, the strangest of all was the boy, for even though a boy, he already had the will of a man. Aristotle saw the young genius of Alexander, real gold, real fire. He pointed to the dangers of combat, the cruelty of fate, the vicissitudes of government, the goal of philosophy. But so long as he could not tell the boy why they were there and to what end, the boy followed his own inclination, which was war. Thus spoke the Wise One. And so began our education.

The prodigy programs were full of kids whose parents had drilled into them that they were a supercomputer or a sacred fire or something still more alarming. But not your son and daughter-in-law. They generally avoided mention of Hannah's gift.

The speed at which things blurred for Hannah was, however, faster than they could see, and they made no secret of it. Some things, like ice-skating, Hannah learned like any child. Others, like higher mathematics, she learned very differently. The more she thought in numbers, the more she intuited their spaces, and soon her mathematical interlocutors were all adults. The Wise One said that Hannah had a special eye and ear for pattern, for the structure, rhythm, regularity and recurrence of pattern. She solved a rubik's cube in thirty-seven seconds because she saw its pattern differently from the next person, who finished in 2:12, which was an entire day faster than third place. And with this the Wise One, the only one of your family who had tasted the bitter fruit of precociousness, was to work.

Your brother's initial instruction consisted of myths, long, complicated, intricate myths, Inuit, Haida, Greek. He would tell us Norse myths full of fire, Hindu myths full of change, Polynesian myths, Malaysian myths, Egyptian myths, myths from the Congo, the Amazon, the Himalayas, from anywhere his mind came to rest. We were unsure if there was invention in his telling, in part because he said myths always had an edge of invention, that's what kept them sharp. When he would finish a myth we were told to interpret it. If we look for terms in which to say who is right then the game is no fun, for it will surely be that it is the feathers of the red horn-bill which are sacred to the creator, not those of the spotted hornbill. We were instructed to listen more imaginatively. To our interpretations he responded first by improving them, strengthening them in all sorts of ways we had never thought of, such that for a moment it seemed you might be righter than you ever knew, and how nice was that. Then came the turn. Hannah called it the thousand knives of reason. When we claimed it was excessive he was quiet a moment, his body stilled by reflection, looking out the window of that room filled with all those books, all those wise things, and at last said: It is the house in flames that truly reveals its architecture.

We snuck into his study one day, to the long desk covered with all that writing, strange objects holding in place the different piles of notes, scraps, sketches, drawings, receipts with notes to self in Latin. Hannah, mesmerized by the wild paraphernalia of erudition, pored over his handwriting, watching how it changed from calm observation to compressed realization to a running cursive afraid of being left behind. When your brother caught us—for, as you know, he had a certain stealth—he sat us down and said that there had been no need to sneak in, we could come whenever we liked, the key was in a drawer of the cabinet outside. But the interesting thing is not there, he said, gesturing to the desk, but here, and he pointed with slow force at the thousands of books, row upon row, shelf upon shelf, rising to the high ceiling. Some see the world as something that rolls right over you, he said, like a wave. Some see it as a gigantic juggernaut of wreckage and harm. And so some see books as an escape, things invented so as to be able to bear the weight of the world. That is no way to see things, he said. The world is wonderful beyond compare. And the lesson of all those books can never be that there exists a model for how to be. Nor can we find in them a reliable record of what has happened. All that is hazy in the extreme. He handed me a small paperweight, surprisingly heavy, raw brass, shaped like a house. While it is true that none of those books can tell you how to live, there are two that come close. Then the Wise One began to read to us, in ancient Greek, and we could tell from everything about the way he spoke and moved that he loved it, and from the movements he made that it was about pride, and thus about conflict.

From that day forward Hannah studied ancient Greek. Wrapped in her father's peacoat, outside, under a tree, before a fire, in bed, at the table, in school. In Greece it had been very bright for a time, very clear, and so many new things were visible that a new question arose, the question of clarity. When your brother reached his limit in thinking something through he would say, cheerfully, something Greek, something I'm not sure you heard. *Everything is fire.* With Hannah it became a greeting and when they would pass one another he would say, casually, *everything is fire,* and Hannah would reply that everything was fire indeed. It was their *ciao.*

The Wise One was not your brother for nothing, as he often said. All feel lack. However much of anything anyone might have, there is always something lacking to their glory. Unless, he said, picking up the first book he had given us, you are like him, like Odysseus. The Wise One had begun our education with *The Odyssey* because he deemed it the more age-appropriate of the Homeric epics, with its monsters and witches and abundance of magic. What it would have been to see him, the Wise One said, to look in Odysseus's warm bemused moving eyes, bright and alert, seeing you, calculating your outcomes. I imagine them dark, like my sister's, he said, pools of night, seeing all. Odysseus had a gift, the thing that Athena so loves about him, that so delights her that he becomes her favorite mortal thing to watch, so endlessly inventive, imaginative, articulate, and winning a man, not just with strength and speed but with his constant calm exploration of the given. Odysseus knew his way was unique, and never tried to make Agamemnon or Ajax or Achilles see things as he did, it being perfectly sufficient for them to see things as he wanted them to. But to his son, with his own, he taught the art of being like him, many-minded, a man of angles, of violence and vengeance, whether a horse for Troy or a banquet for those he was about to kill.

The Wise One told us that some did not like Odysseus. He told us that Dante put him in hell. Which gives you a sense of why people call them the dark ages, he said. Why Virgil described him darkly is because the Romans hated him for the Horse. The Wise One told us that this was silly, for without the fall of Troy there would have been no refugees from Troy, and thus no need for Venus's son to prance around the Mediterranean organizing gymnastic spectacles. Without Odysseus the Trojan prince Aeneas would have stayed right at home in Troy with, as result, no Rome. But the important question, he said, is the Horse. Dante punishes Odysseus for the trickery of it. Of course it was a trick. It was a war. Shields are tricks. Swords are tricks, chariots and horses and helmets and siege engines and elephants and fire are all tricks. The Romans believed they descended from the Trojans and so inherited their hostilities. But the truth is that there was no violation of ancient rule in the Horse. About this your brother was categorical. *How do you get through impregnable walls?* is a question with a real answer. You have the people inside wheel you in and then go to bed. If you are Odysseus. And thereby your brother gave your grand-daughter the idea for your fall, just as one day he would give her the keys to your city.

We thought it a bit beneath the Wise One to teach us, or to teach anyone. We felt he should be off making neutrinos, building spaceships, mastering the heavens. When Hannah asked why he didn't make a book out of all those notes, all the piles of writing on his long desk, he said that Odysseus would never have written *Notions of Intentionality in Kantian Epistemology*. Hannah said that he would have climbed in a boat and sailed somewhere and then either something magical would have happened or he would have killed somebody. The Wise One said she was quite right. One way of winning in life, he said, is to contend with all manner of obstacles, challenges, situations and persons, and to have your way. Another is to be content with everything it falls to you to encounter, flocks of starlings at dusk, a shantytown bathroom opening onto the void, baroque cathedrals, mountains, the wide Pacific. No one is watching through your eyes but you, he said. You might make this fact lonely, cold, dark, frightening. Or you might use your unique line of sight to think of what you want and bring it to pass. For you can demand all you like, stamp your feet and not come down to dinner, but the world has never given in, never given up its secret, except in the form of divine intervention, which has always ended badly, with bushes on fire and people nailed to things.

Your brother spoke in such terms whenever Hannah came home from one of your family visits to Church. Cold elegant adoration of the divinity, she said he said. She had found it amazing, and as soon as she got home went searching for a Bible. She spent all day with it, and the next and the next, which your daughter-in-law mistook for the first flickerings of faith. Hannah came over with the huge book in her arms and we read parts of it together. It was unbelievable. A good bit of it flat-out terrifying. Adults mass-circumcising themselves, babies in bulrushes, plague, magical seas, rain of frogs, Assyrian warlords, the End of Days. Like most children, we could relate to the Old Testament deity, but not the New. We agreed that Jesus sounded like an extremely fun person. One day the Wise One found Hannah at his desk with his largest and oldest Bible. Real whodunit, he said. The end is repetitive, she said. They keep killing Jesus. He asked if she had other observations and she said that she thought the Gospels would be better if they ended with the death of Jesus. The way he comes back is so unlike him, she said. She also said that she felt bad for Cain. Sure, he behaved terribly, she said, but think about his upbringing. The worst thing that would ever happen happened to his parents, their eyes still full of Eden, their minds ravaged by its loss, and they never had parents and so were not likely to know what they were doing even under the best of circumstances. The Unnamable was in no mood to offer assistance. Poor Cain, she said. His blood was washed away in the Flood, the Wise One replied, and they continued through the generations.

The world, the Wise One said, is a perfect locked-door mystery (he knew Hannah had recently read "The Murders in the Rue Morgue" and was in the habit of comparing murder by orangutan to the most varied things). How did we get in here, what is here, is there an outside of here, who the fuck are all these people, are all, he said, questions without answer. The most consistently rewarding path has been calm in the storm. It has been to think of nothing. The few who have learned to think of nothing have realized they were thinking of death, which promptly ceased to frighten them. The Buddha, Socrates, and a great many other wise ones became quite cheerful about death at that moment. Egyptians, Persians, Greeks, Romans, Carthaginians, Jews, Christians, Muslims all wanted order, needed order, had a story about order, its nature, its beginning, and some strict rules to be followed for the future, generally involving the notion that if you kill animals in precise ways and offer to God the parts you don't want then everything will be fine. For a time.

The Greeks, he said, imagined that their gods had not less but more extreme tastes than men. They were so fiercely proud that they killed mortals who even suggested they might play a musical instrument as well as a god. They were, in a word, children. For what could have aged them? A god is a force, imagined as a person, the Wise One said. Imagining the god as being like a person, as having the shape of a person, only larger and immortal, with a smithy under Mount Etna, is not so strange. Those who paid tribute to Hephaestus were respecting not a cranky giant filling commissions for Olympus who was busy and strong and dirty and swore a lot. That is not what a god is to a thinking member of a community. They were worshipping a human capacity and a social necessity, he said. But the same is not true of my sister's god. He is jealous.

Hannah's only strong theological position at the time concerned killer whales. We, of course, came to know most things you knew, reading your email, listening to your conversations, studying you, tracking you, hunting you. But I don't know what you know of Hannah's young travels, it not having been relevant to your ruin. As a girl, during the Divide, Hannah had been in a kayak in Vancouver Sound with her mother. It was fresh and still and they were paddling along and then the sea rose and there it was, its fin high and huge. And everything, Hannah said, about its arrival and presence was incredibly powerful, and yet calm, reassuring, even polite. And yet, she said, they kill absolutely everything else in the sea. They eat whales, she said. They eat great white sharks. They are not called killer for nothing. They kill everything. Fish, seals, sea lions, otters, walruses, notwithstanding the tusks, dolphins, notwithstanding the cuteness. They even kill bears and moose if they find them in the water. And yet to us they are kind. Not only has there never been a case of a free-swimming killer whale killing a person, there has never been one of a killer whale even harming one. On the contrary, Hannah said. They lead boats out of fog. They return dogs lost at sea. The Haida, the people who live on the boundary of the worlds, think they are gods, she said, and I think they are right.

Among all the many myths told us, those the Wise One had us contemplate, there was one he left out. When Hannah found it, on her own, among his books, she was angry, for she considered it the best. Achilles was so loved by his mother, the nymph Thetis, that she could not bear what she knew, could not bear to see him die young, die barely a boy in her eyes. Even if he lived a hundred years he would be a boy in her eyes, would always live only a moment, but she could not resist the desire for it to last, and so she presented him with an inhuman choice. She came to him, as she always had, in the sea, and told him that he might live in tranquil happiness to a great age, beloved of children and grandchildren, a king honored by all, then forgotten. Or he could sail to Troy, fight more gloriously than any mortal ever, and so breathtaking and beautiful would it be that so long as men spoke of war they would speak of him. In which case he would die young. Hannah told the story breathlessly, repeatedly, to many, even Sedna.

Her cheeks flushed when she got to the part where Achilles, after his mother has presented the choices, does not hesitate, does not take refuge in her arms, but simply gathers his things, assembles his men, and sails, sacking cities on the way until he arrives before the high walls of Troy, ready.

Hannah told me of the day you noticed she would be beautiful. You noticed it casually, she said, and then turned all your attention on her, as never before, and it frightened her an instant, she said, you had such directness in your gaze, like she had never seen, that you were like no one she had ever seen, your dark eyes all attention. A moment later you were mild again, distant. In your rich rough voice you spoke of her beauty, not to praise her, for that would make no sense, it not having been any of her doing. You told her that she was going to need to learn something not everyone knew because not everyone needed to. There are people who regard beauty as though it were a public good, you said, like a national park or a magical bird, something of which you are less the possessor than the custodian. They will think you owe them access. Nothing is sillier, you said. It is silly to speak about beauty as anything other than a gift, and with a gift you may do as you like. You told her that before long turning the full glare of her beauty on someone would be enough to change the situation. It is with beauty that you always begin, you said, it is always through the door first. So be careful how you use it, careful how you think about it. You must never make it a single fact, because if there were simply two states, beautiful and not, every new encounter would be a referendum on the question, instead of being what it truly is, which is individual and surprising. You told her that to be desired by all would be tiresome. When she told your wise brother your words he said, think how her God must feel. No wonder he acts out like he does. The Fruit, the Flood, the Sacrifice, the mass circumcision all show signs of capricious exasperation. Precisely what a universally desired being would be liable to feel. You do not want to be universally desired, the Wise One told Hannah. It is not lacking to your glory.

Your lawyers stressed your demand for all information concerning the other grand-daughter involved in your family's fall. For all I know you love Annika dearly. You may be aware of her deeds and her nature and love her all the same, or all the more. Like every other person ever she did not ask to be as she is. And yet then again she did some pretty remarkable things to you. Were it not for your wealth and the indolence it encouraged, I think Annika would have become something competitive. A dancer. A rhythmic gymnast. A biathlete. An assassin. She is amazingly good in motion. And has for all intents and purposes no moral reservations, at least as far as I was able to see, which was far. The Wise One said that many people have demented moral codes full of arbitrary exemptions. Thou shalt not kill, unless the person has different dietary restrictions, unless they believe the father came before the son, unless they are wearing red. Annika's moral flexibility was of a different sort. It was fundamental. Order had some basic claim on me, on Hannah, such that we would seek it, whereas Annika was truly amphibious about order. She could move about it for a time, enjoying its benefits, appreciating its rhythms, and then one day she would see the sea and crave disorder like an animal craves water and she would run right for it down the long stretch of sand, stripping off clothes as she went, until she dove into the icy waters, not icy to her.

When she learned about anarchists in school Annika could not believe that everyone with a choice wasn't one. It baffled her. Many broke rules because the rules were between them and what they wanted. Annika broke them because they were rules. Hannah was so fast in mind that the more movement there was in a situation the greater her advantage. Except with her cousin. Annika she could not read, could not control, could not predict. Her moves were too strange. Annika could have thought of the Trojan horse, the Wise One observed, such was her marrying of the bizarre and the lethal.

The sound must have woke me, must have woke everything. Annika was to recall passing the statue of a warrior and returning his frown. She was to remember the darkened library and the anger and the alcohol slowing for a moment as she thought of being small and looking up at the giant mural with the red-bearded giant wading through clear mountain waters and then there was the tree. Everything was quiet. Shocked. Resonating. I heard the ticking of metal, the rustling of leaves, the cicadas resume. Then I heard her. I went to Gaby's room, pushed aside her night table and smelled marijuana. My sister was not going to get into Harvard like this. A breeze lifted the leaves and I saw, as in a dream, an elfin-beautiful and orc-drunk Annika berating a tree. She abused the tree she had smashed into. She demanded that it account for itself, asked how it dared, what it thought it was doing there, at such an hour. I remember the lights of a police car lighting up the leaves and that as Annika was firmly placed in the police car she looked up through the night, through the drunkenness, and winked.

Annika returned so close to the onset of adolescence that the more superstitious thought of her as its cause. She sat next to me in algebra. She had a cut above her eye from the accident. She had been gone for years, your nephew having sent her to boarding school in response to what her school conduct file called precocious malfeasance. She dressed very punk rock with rips and tears and indifferent revelations. Being so close to such a large university meant our school was humane and our teachers all caring in one well-meaning if futile way or another. Several had doctorates and all seemed smart and melancholy. All except our algebra teacher, who was also a football coach, and happy. We were very bad at football and routinely lost by unrealistic scores, ones that seemed to belong to a different, higher-scoring sport, like cricket. This football-loving and losing teacher had been called upon to replace someone at the last minute. He was not good at math. We saw that he was teaching, unlike our other teachers, and examining, unlike our other teachers, from a standard textbook. We took the catalog belonging to the mother of a friend who taught at another school and ordered the instructor's copy of the book he was using, complete with answers, watched the mail carefully for its arrival, and dispensed with further study. One day, befuddled by Annika's sudden success, and provoked by a large hole in her Crucifucks t-shirt, he stopped before us and looked and looked and shook his head. Suddenly confronted by what we spent every day with—the mystery of her—he was confused. He asked Annika what she wanted to be when she grew up. She beamed, saying nothing for a long time, gazing dreamily out the window, before at last turning on him, holding him, knowing where his gaze had been, and said she would become a French porn star. After he walked away, his pedagogical fire spent, I whispered, But you're not French. You don't know how to listen, she said, and threw one of her legs over mine.

I think I have a run in my stocking, she said in the crisp English accent of her boarding school. A big one. A few minutes later she said, Put your hand on my leg. I can't do math without a hand on my leg. Its heat was amazing. She was like a small furnace. We were all like small furnaces. All mankind furnaces, but none so furnace as Annika. Feel that tear? she asked. Do you know how far it goes? Do you want to find out? I said that they could see. The real question, she said, is can Hannah?

My sexual relations, as your lawyers' questionnaire calls them, with Annika began at your birthday party, and thus virtually in your presence. Hannah, Annika and I were received at your most impressive ancestral estate by your eldest, Sixten the Strong. You were engaged with dignitaries of what Hannah called dubious aspect. Turning away from them, Sixten Syrl looked from the balcony of his forefathers and said, *The cicadas don't care*. He seemed to feel that he was showing good breeding and displaying enlightened views in allowing other people to be around him at all. Even Annika was impressed. A man that can stand on a 17th century balcony staring out over lands stretching to the horizon which have belonged to his family for as long as anyone could remember and still want the cicadas to care is, as she conceded, extraordinary.

He knew what Hannah must have thought of him, knew that his youngest brother had lived long enough to hand down his hostility. So he presented himself in an unusual light. Aristocracy, like any other form of hereditary advantage, he said, is phenomenally unjust by any moral standard. And it has existed everywhere at every point of recorded history. Descendents of the Raven Spirit, Shaman of the Night, High Priest of Nineveh, Holy Roman Emperor, Dauphin of France, all one, he said. The question is then what your position should be if you find yourself, if you wake up to the world, privileged? Should you reject it on principle as an unfair result? As a mere child should you know to do this? And if you do, will they not simply find another Shaman of the Night? Privilege is a function of fortune, he said, and fortune a function of property and property, if you go back far enough, is just who was first, the people here longest, whoever they are, being better, as time has shown. Aristocracy is thus a matter of time. It is a great and noble thing for an Englishman to have come over with the Conqueror. Why? He was a French Viking and his army of French Vikings invaded, unprovoked, the British Isles and subjugated them not with fine French wines, women, food and art, but with fire, blood, rape, and murder. Vikings, Sixten said, are famous not for sculpture or painting or music or mathematics or architecture or aqueducts or poetry or anything but the long boats they used to reach distant locations and the harm they brought when they came ashore in them. These were terrifically destructive people, essentially illiterate, and yet now the English are as proud as can be to descend from them, and still look down on the descendants of the peaceful peasants and artisans who were harvesting crops and teaching one another to read when the Vikings arrived. Which poses the question of wealth. Its answer is this, he said, with endless variations, all of them exciting, all of it a grand game.

Sixten told us how archaeologists had found nearby the site of a thousand-year-old massacre, seventy-three adult men, clad in armor, beheaded in a row. The archaeologist who found them started to study the vertebrae, he said, and saw that they were wrong, the marks were wrong, they could only have been made from the front, and so thought they must be fakes. At which point, said Sixten, along came an archaeologist who knew Vikings, and informed him that they were perfectly real. Captured Vikings accepted to be put to death in only one position: standing, facing the blade, eyes open. They would not flinch. We are a fundamentally frightening people, Sixten said, on that point the historical record is clear. He told us that the Syrls were different from the other families of their fjords in one principal regard: vengeance. It had always been the great ambition of your family to be renowned for vengefulness. He said that in the Icelandic saga where you are first mentioned a monk says that when you watch the Syrls, they watch back, together, like wolves. Of this Sixten was proud. He said that you stayed true to your origins, that while other families became interested in things like silk breeches and whist, you kept to the seas, that you joined a banking venture in time to get a shiny gold ticket to a very long ball. In the history of the family there was, your son made clear, a range of Syrlness, and thus an ideal of Syrlness, and that from time to time a child was born who would be recognized as being particularly Syrl, as having all of the essential traits, something treasured by all. To Hannah he said that he was such a Syrl, and that she was such another.

The sheer ursine power, as Hannah called it, of your eldest son was impressive, especially in his element. He explained what he knew best, the codified world of your weekends, where no one could go home before the princess, people no one may address otherwise than in the third person, the last ramparts of civility. All that adulation of ancestry, all that archaic intensity of feeling is now visible only in restraint, he said, your cardinal virtue. You dressed like others, only a little finer wool, softer cotton, more elegant cut, but nothing to stand out, not a garment made entirely of gold, not the head of a lion, not a sword of ancient manufacture, all serene, Sixten said, we are all serene.

Our family imperative is simple, he said. Rule. Nothing more complicated. We decide our destiny and if people have to starve for that to happen it would not have been our idea, for we did not create the order of things. What happens to those at the end of my sword is their own bad luck, he said, is the way of the world, is the night of time. Attempts to change the order have been many, he said, and failures. He pointed to my feet and said that to sew shoes in an infernal place, no air and all sweat and chemical and mind-numbing machines, is humanly terrible in every way. The world is full of fates, he said, and countless ones at this moment of history are terrible, as at all moments of history. I know that families live in a mangrove forest where tigers kill people, but how relevant is that for my evening? The secret to wealth, Sixten said, the one my little brother never learned, lies in not mistaking it for something else. The rich are not happier than the poor. Or less happy. They are differently happy, corresponding to their different way of life. If you have little and suddenly are given much, money proves wonderful, proves a delight, for as long as it lasts. This is why the poor think they see through wealth, he said, why they think that they understand it entire. I grant that from afar it seems simple enough. We have more than we need, they not enough, it's not rocket science. Until you start to do what your father did, said Sixten, turning to Hannah. What if you tell them to come up whenever they like and take from our rich granaries? How does that end? Do they just take a cup, a bag, what they need? Do they form a utopian collective equitably distributing privilege, resources, and grain, free of ambition, cleansed by the waters of poverty? Or do they tear one another apart like on every other occasion in the history of mankind? If we did it would be one large loud destructive fight with the end worse than the beginning. Think of China, he said. And grow up. Sixten Syrl then looked into the distance, straightened his elegant suit, forgave the cicadas, and went inside.

Once the festivities were over, with the cool of evening moving up the hill, flowing from the forest, I wandered outside to see your famous tree. I had always admired the simplicity of your coat of arms, no rampant lions or bears or swords uplifted, no gules or sable, just the tree. I walked down to it, the grass wet with dew, and sat beneath it, feeling it stretch above me, old. You would have been holding court inside. The formal part of the party was over. At such events Hannah had to hear many unpleasant things about her father, and she had gone off to talk to the Wise One about him, your brother being the family expert on the subject of disinheritance. I was looking at the statue, Roman, imperial, arm raised in calm dominion, giving something to the people, like life. I thought it amazing that he had no head. The Wise One told us that many statues had replacement heads. He said your decision to leave it as found was a better one. More revealing, he said.

Annika found me by the tree. I think people often desire her before their eyes have time to focus. They feel a wave of her warmth, a gentle blurring of the light in which her beauty grows clear. She smelled unusual and when you got closer it deepened and darkened and drew. She slipped a shoulder free of its strap, gracefully, and she said, I know you. You belong to Hannah. I belong to me, I said. Then would you like to see the grounds? The orangerie? There are no oranges there, she said. There are other things.

When we returned it was night. The House of Syrl glowed from afar, the emperor offering his headless protection, giving his headless command. Syrls strolled the manicured grounds, roamed the rooms, celebrating themselves. Annika and I chose separate entrances. I felt elation and concern. I had never had sex with anyone but Hannah. I remember wishing I could talk to Hannah about it. I looked over at Annika, her face visible in the light from the house. She winked.

I had kissed someone else. One bleary night I walked into a room at a smoky, humid party and she kissed me, open-mouthed and warm on the lips. I wondered if she mistook me for someone else and I kissed back. When I told Hannah the next morning she laughed, which proved a misleading precedent. For when I told her about Annika she was standing in my room, next to a bust of Plato, a thing I loved, his head so solid, cast by a German in another century, not valuable, but with value to me, and she raised it high and smashed it into a thousand little Platos. I never bore her any ill will for what she did next, or the scar it left.

The answer to your lawyers' question concerning sexual relation with Hannah is a year earlier. There were isolated ponds in the woods and Hannah and I had gone to the most remote of them. Trees grew right up to its edge, hanging over the water, the shallows dark. At the far end was a small sandy sunny beach. It was hot and the sun shone through the leaves. I had no bathing suit. Hannah looked at me, laughed brightly, darkly, said I was silly, began to undress.

Nothing you haven't seen before, she said. Which was true and false.

First one to the beach wins.

What do we win?

Whatever we want, she said with a shrug, and, naked in the sunlight, ran and dove.

I undressed fast, hoping I could get into the water before she surfaced. I heard her an instant before I hit the water. I stayed under as long as I could, the water cool, clear, concealing. Hannah had drifted into the sun, her eyes full of it. She let me get close, swam away, then back, and suddenly her mouth was on mine, differently than before. Her body slid against mine and her eyes shone mischief and she was too close to see and there was water and she was slippery and warm in the cold and her breasts were against me and sinking and rising, slipping and kicking, and the water and the tingling and the pressing and then my foot touched bottom and something happened which had never happened before.

The next day the phone in the kitchen rang and I answered it. *Why don't you come over and fuck me.* It was for me. I rode my bike as fast as I could, lungs afire, and twenty minutes later, sitting in a patch of sunlight, her weight on me, Hannah whispered something surprising in my ear. She told me I hadn't been supposed to react as I did. So we tried again. Regularly.

We found it scarcely believable that it took place in the world, that the world had kept such a secret, that it had managed to conceal such a glowing thing.

Given our position on adult authority it is unsurprising that we were caught a number of times and in a number of places. In classrooms, the gymnasium, among the dustiness at the back of the theater, in the botanical garden, in the soundproofed practice rooms of the music building, in the natural history museum in front of a diorama of megafauna watching with what Hannah called prehistoric approval. We were surprised by both of my parents, on separate occasions, as well as by your daughter-in-law. My father wasn't meant to be home and he came home and the music was turned up, and he came in to have me turn it down, or so he said, though he probably wasn't lying. Loud music annoyed him. In a surprisingly calm voice he told us to get dressed and come downstairs. He told Hannah, not unkindly, that it was best if she went home, and she did. His first question to me was: Were you wearing a condom? When my mother caught us her first question was: Do you love her? My mother, though, had an additional question. She asked whether your daughter-in-law knew and I said I didn't know. Do you think she has a right to know? I said no. How do you think she would feel if she knew? I said I thought she would be upset (this proved correct).

Why would she be upset?

Because parents get upset about it.

Do you think I'm upset?

You don't look upset but I don't know.

It was clear she was balancing principles, just as it was clear that she was absorbing a new fact, a fundamental fact, premature but wished for, that her son first know sex as love. My mother may not have been an ideal mother from the reliability standpoint, but she had a good heart. And notwithstanding her relationship with your son, she seems to have had a very healthy view of sex. Maybe notwithstanding is not the word.

When nowhere else was available, we, like our ancestors, took to the woods and the lakes. We capsized a rowboat. We got suspiciously placed poison oak that required medical attention. Years later, when our war against you had begun, we were in Rome and walked by a Roman presenting his city to a group of people. He said *Questo è il colosseo*. And then he turned around towards Rome stretching away with its ruins and its churches and its columns and said *E questo è il non-colosseo*. Our world was divided between coliseum and non-coliseum. Until Annika.

Annika loved sex to an amazing degree, and in some amazing ways, including many that I had not known existed. This had less to do with my lack of imagination, or Hannah's, than with Annika's fundamental creativity in the matter. I was leaving a school party, moving through the crowd with your son's peacoat over my shoulder. It had a hook to hold the collar closed in the face of a gale, as you might remember, for you bought it for him, and as I wove my way across the dance floor I felt it catch. I turned so as not to tear delicate fabric and saw a familiar face. Look what you caught, said Annika. Then she resumed dancing and with her eyes and her arms and every playful angling of her body said that it was time to play, that she was good at playing, that she couldn't wait to play. The force was strong in her, as her little brother once said, wearing a cape.

The next morning Annika and I drove up the coast. It was hot and deserted and there was no one on the trails. We hadn't seen anyone in an hour. She had taken off everything but her underwear and hiking boots. We saw a small black bear in the distance and waved. We made our way down from the cliff to a bluff and from the bluff to the beach. I felt cool air and warmth not mine. Annika's eyes grew dreamy and focused, pushing me down, pushing down through me. She had exceptionally lovely breasts. The prominence of her hip bones had a golden mean. Her shoulders and collarbones were highly expressive. These things I thought as we lay, sand-abraded, and she asked about Hannah.

That's strange, she said. You should be true to your strongest feeling, not your oldest bond. You owe it to the moment to make it as bright as possible, for they are few, as the Wise One says, even if they are many. Annika too had learned from your wise brother. And he from her. Annika's belief was that the world was far simpler than those around her were willing to accept. For her, physical attraction was the decisive motor of all human event. It was her reality to such an extent that she believed it to be everyone's. She often refused to believe that anyone genuinely thought any other way about it, which meant that she saw most people as wildly hypocritical about sexual matters. When she found herself among philosophers it was different, however. For theirs was not hypocrisy. She would move among them, old and young, at receptions, at her father's lectures, transfixed. They were for her like a remote tribe in their singularity, strangeness and confusion considering the fundamental forces at play. She saw the possibility that they might actually believe what they were saying, that everything is mind. And seeing that they were incapable of acting on their desires in a time-sensitive manner, she showed them the way. She watched their terror before the reality of offer, watched them see that a desire like hers did not have to be passed through committees and subcommittees before acquiring a mandate for action. And they could not imagine that their confusion and awkwardness were attractive, that it was exciting for her to help those so out of touch with their desires they had had to invent philosophy to console themselves, the poor things.

Annika almost never referred to anything she read, and read very little, as far as I could tell. But she once told me about a book the Wise One had given her where some writer, she didn't remember who, said that true happiness would be a charming little house with a garden and a view of a valley and an orchard with a row of seven trees from which hung your seven worst enemies alongside your seven best friends. Annika seemed to understand with unnerving clarity the part about the friends. It is not uncommon for someone to radiate power, but to radiate anarchy, to radiate irreverence, as did Annika, is rare in the extreme, as the Wise One confirmed. When her sun was out Annika was tropical. It did not look frenetic or forced, it just looked like more, more life and joy and desire. One moment it would be summer in full force and flower and things were wonderful such that anything else seemed a dream, an aberration, a winter that would never come again. And then the generator would go out, like the power outages in Caracas, grid after grid, the huge city going dark, the whole valley green in the moonlight, the insects loud, spreading the word that something bad was on its way. Annika's own father compared her to the roaring 40s, the southernmost latitudes, so far south that they circle the entire watery world without ever touching land, and because those waves circle the entire planet without ever breaking, they are as high as skyscrapers, they are of a terrifying size and violence, they are the principal obstacle to anyone trying to sail around the world, for once you dip below the line of land, into the roaring 40s, you find yourself in them very quickly and nothing prepares you and they kill almost everyone, one way or another. And to them he compared his only daughter.

The psychoanalysis, in the words of Annika's analyst, did not take. It seemed to her that psychoanalysis encourages you to see your child self as different, to see it as though from the outside, and to assess its situation, understand its pain and fear and world, see the extent to which that pain and those fears were justified in that world, and then to bend down over the child in yourself and tell it you are proud of it, that it has fought bravely, valiantly, for all these years, with ingenuity and ferocity, and that the war is over, it can rest, at last, and put down the sword. But whenever anyone told Annika to put down her sword, her first response was to run them through with it. As you well know.

The answer to your next question is that Justin entered our lives at this time. During the first storms of sex my mind would move through the new spaces and I would find myself imagining all manner of things. And every once in a while an image would drift through my mind as Hannah and I had sex of Hannah having sex with another. Never a known person. But also not me. And so when Justin arrived I wondered whether I had not somehow called him into being, like a golem. For as Hannah came of sexual age there was a revolution in behavior towards her, at the head of which rode Justin. I didn't blame him. Who could better understand interest in Hannah than I? Though I did fight him. I was like a monk lighting himself on fire, said Gaby during one of her visits. Extreme protest at the cost of great physical harm, this was the Old Way. I remember that the punches Justin threw were not a child's punches. They were a foretaste of adulthood. And he was going easy, although I wouldn't know it until months later when I saw him respond to a real threat. Before the college football player finished his sentence Justin rammed the butt of his hand into his throat, collapsing the windpipe, kneed him in the balls, landed a punch of dangerous downward angle, and in a single smooth movement grabbed his skateboard, whirled and hit him with it, hard, making a sickening noise. Justin was exemplary.

The first time I heard about Justin was from Gaby, home for the summer. Hannah was there and asked Gaby what he was like, where he was from in California, and Gaby replied that he had eyes like embers, and hers glowed an instant. He's beautiful. And big, she said. I remember watching the cat, Ming, lick his genitals with serene focus. I had heard enough.

Justin was not like his brother, who was doubtless beautiful—and whose success with girls reflected this—but whose beauty was delicate and fragile, such that women wanted to touch it and men to break it. Justin was different. His beauty was not fragile. Nor did he treat it as such. On the contrary, he routinely exposed it to harm. I would have been happy to hate Justin. I remember Gaby holding my head to the light, studying the cut his first punch had made. What did you think, she asked, that Hannah would never touch anyone but you? That was indeed what I thought. Gaby cleaned my cut the Old Way, having Sedna lick it, and as she fixed the butterfly suture in place said, If you look at it like a contest, one where you and Justin are competing, then this is not a great moment for you. So don't look at it like that.

A few weeks later Gaby came into my room to inquire about some splintered wood she had found outside. Wow, she said when I told her what I had seen, what had been done, with what I had to live. She pushed my feet to the side and lay down on the bed. Gaby was already tall and took up a lot of space. Sedna came in, looked at the unusual configuration, and got on the bed too, and as Gaby talked and talked I remembered the first hazy moments of having a sister. The world, big, chaotic, menacing, was waiting outside and I listened to the leaves, the katydids, to Sedna's soft snore, and to my sister tell me what I knew. I knew that every relationship was different not just in degree but kind. I knew that every bond was unique and had unique forms of expression. I knew that much misfortune comes from comparison. I knew that sexual possession was not the word for it. I knew that turnabout was fair play. But it took my breath away all the same. Gaby fell asleep. She slept like our mother, her breathing slowing, growing deeper, until skipping a beat in its long glide downwards. Just before Gaby entered the last chamber of sleep she said that it would be fine, just not right away.

One day Hannah and I got into a loud fight in Greek and were sent home. I remember walking through the woods, the light all uncertain, cold, wishing Sedna was there and walking up the stairs to the glass house, the green of the hedges protecting me, smelling pine and resin and rain, and I wanted to stay away forever so as to show Hannah how it felt.

She was in the kitchen and saw me before I knocked. I watched her cheeks flush, her brow turn fierce, her back straighten, her eyes burn. She was barefoot and walked across the floor in long strides, opened the glass door slowly, formally. And as I stepped inside she let go. She lifted my arms, opened my shirt and hers, and pressed her chest against mine, slowly, like a ritual. I said that the Greeks had no word for peace, only one for truce. Then we should say it in English, she said, and ran her finger next to my eye, along the cut. I'll let you know when I want you to fight for me, she said. Which, in the fullness of time, she did.

The answer to your lawyers' next question, that of when Hannah began her war against you, you know better than all. It began the moment it ended. She did not tell me at first. At the airport her eyes were clouded. Her eyes said: I know, I hear the static, I might be the static, but whatever it is do not make me talk about it. Hannah was strange and insisted that we drive, far, that we drive west, said that the

Wise One had arranged it, that it was fine with everyone, just drive. People who drive across the country are routinely shocked by the middle. It is, as Hannah said, very fat, and loves loud powerful things like weapons and monster trucks and even its ways of being religious are magical and violent and it mesmerized her. The farther west we went the flatter it became, and the more incredible. Until at last we saw the Rockies. We stayed in a high canyon all white and blue. We went down the Grand Staircase, canyon after canyon. We stood in a huge valley, broad from below, narrow from above, and looked up at the soaring walls of rock so high that the trees at its rim were miniscule and Hannah talked about the river that had made the valley, how we were in the giant bed of what was once a river of such prehistoric violence that it made the valley, a million million years, every moment taking a grain of rock downstream for more moments than a mind can imagine. Maybe this is what the Amazon will be like one day in a million years when killer whales rule the earth, she said.

We found a place where the current was fast, the snowmelt like ice after the fiery air, and we slipped downstream to the rapids and held on to the rocks, our bodies pulled long by the current. Hannah looked at me underwater, her hair floating, her eyes wide, and I saw her look change, release, relax, and turn furious. When we climbed out she was quiet, in the car she was quiet, driving through the orange and the red desert, the land unearthly with spikes and spires and strangenesses, quiet. As the setting sun made the red rock glow she began. Her voice was raspy at first. I'll tell you the static, she said. But you have to drive. There was nothing but desert and no cars in sight. So long as you drive I tell. You stop I stop. And if I stop I won't be able to restart.

I could hear that she had never told it before and so every detail was like a decision. She told of the room full of books with the swallows darting and the dusk deepening and how amazing it all was. She talked of your ancestral home, how large, how solid, how old, how every time she visited it she liked it more, found different rooms from which to see the tree, salute the emperor, consider the Vikings, how she could imagine wanting it, as did all in your family, full as it was of stories, full as it was of time. She told me about the library built by your father. She said that many were warm to her, told her she looked like her father, looked like a Syrl, that she was welcome.

It was a humid night, she said, barely cooler than the day, and it was beginning to happen. She told of the dinner, the speeches, Sixten's plan, Sixten's challenge, Sixten's situation. She knew what I had seen, and what you had not, for you only saw the second time Hannah humiliated your eldest son in public. I saw the first. Your eldest thought that if his niece, the special one, seconded him, his ascension would be certain, the rift closed, his nomination made, his reign secure if even the faraway prodigy thought he was a good idea. As he was envisioning the ways in which she might be useful to him, Hannah suddenly stood and addressed all those Syrls, without their matriarch, but numerous, and so young was she, so seriously did she stand, that all fell silent, and she began to speak.

The ease with which she then undid his arguments, the ease with which she saw how Sixten most wanted to appear, how he most feared appearing, the ease with which she turned your son round his own circles was stunning. She spoke of his plan as one does of something so empty of reason that it is sort of cute and gave degree after degree of extensive cousinage a lesson in how to oppose your famously formidable son. But it was not until he let slip an allusion to her father that she showed him how things stood in the real world, showed Sixten what a keener observer, such as you, would have seen from the outset, which was that Hannah was too many for him. The faraway son, dead young in a strange land, had a still more faraway daughter, and she had come from across the seas to rule. And she continued, her voice warmer and firmer as she took aim at her uncle and released, released, released. When she finished the silence was as total as if she had used real arrows.

And so through the darkening desert, the sky still blue, still unaware of what was below, Hannah told me of a still more surprising, still more important meeting, and how she took your son apart anew. She told me of the dinner, of the toasts, of the talking, of the generalized expectation, all knowing the vote was the next day, and how she felt their curiosity flutter about and come to rest on her, waiting and wondering whether she would speak again. She told me of Sixten's toast, his speech, his plea, his plan. She said that he presented his theory of civilization. Once we stopped being hunter-gatherers we had excess people and we began to use their excess in different ways, to plow fields or build ziggurats or conduct day trading or clean toilets. Nothing has changed, he said, nothing needs to. I will do as my father did before me, and his before him, pointing to the wall with your family tree carved into it. We might interrupt this particular course of action, he said, as some of you ask. But what are the other options? And where do they lead but the end? The price to maintain this house, these lands, is astronomical. The government no longer even bothers to conceal the fact that they want to cancel our privileges, to tax away what has been ours for longer than any of them can imagine. If we do not take the opportunity that has presented itself they will keep coming up the hill until all is gone and we are dead. Hannah summarized his position as: I will be a dog to you and a wolf to them. I will make the winter comfortable and short, the summer green and long. And to do this I need to dig a giant hole in the Amazon, and your approval.

Driving through the darkening desert Hannah told me of the light slanting through the room, the table heavy with silver, the air bright with motes, pollen, summer, of how when the moment presented itself she knew it and stood and her heart raced loud in her ears and her hands trembled as she began to speak in that high old room where her father was made so often to sit so quietly. The reason her second public confrontation with Sixten was even more devastating than the first is simple, for in the meantime Hannah had done some research. And she presented the room, presented Sixten, with a new fact. The whisper of him that went everywhere, the shushivering rumor of his person that was music to his ears, that was the sound for him of victory, that she could silence at will.

Hannah told me of the quiet that followed her speech, of your unreadable eyes, of how many sought her out, smiles at the corners of their mouths as if to say, You are an entertaining creature. You are a remarkable Syrl. She told me of the long milling about and the slow going of ways. She told me of texting with her mother, of texting with me as she strolled through the many rooms, keys in hand, opening doors in the least used wing, turning on lights, uncovering paintings, looking out through the windows at the dark night, enjoying her victory. It was late and she was far and she turned back, and she saw him coming. It was as though it had more heat, she said, the space he was moving through, because there was so much anger in it. As soon as he got close she saw that she had been wrong about him and knowing it was like a high-pitched noise that hurt her ears. She saw that something in him had shifted, something in him was decided, bluntly, like an animal, that he was going to have what the mean, impudent, cruel world withheld. She told of how he went, talking all the while, feigning distraction, feigning relaxation, to the door with the keys still in it, how he locked it, pretending to play a game, but only just.

It began very violently, the physical part. I slowed precipitously. Hannah told me to drive. He saw my answer, she said. Which is to say that he saw that I had understood the question. And I saw that he was locked in. That is the part I hate least, she said, the animal demand of it, she said. What I hate most is the human of it, his eyes interested in the pain, moving through it as through a clearing dappled with sunlight, marveling at what he found in the forest. He could do whatever he liked, here I was not stronger than him, and this was the purest proof of it, for if I were so special how could he be doing as he was. At first he looked right through my eyes, as if dreaming, she said. As he came closer his eyes changed and he grew enchanted by the pain, causing more so as to see more power to cause it. And as he tore into me, she said, a thought grew and grew. As he walked out, replacing the key, he said, If you even whisper of this I'll do worse. And she whispered back that he was wrong.

*   *   *

Hannah fell asleep in the car, a long reddish lock across her forehead, damp with sweat, and I didn't want to wake her, so I drove through the desert all night, wanting speed, wanting blood, so thirsty for it I couldn't swallow. I woke Hannah at dawn, at the ocean, the air fresh with sea-spray. The cabin had been built by a Norwegian long ago, before the land was made a nature preserve. Being older than the park meant it was allowed to stay on the condition it not turn too much of a profit. The Wise One had known how to arrange it. We let Sedna loose in the forest full of strange smells, Californian bears, mountain lions, horses, coyotes. We swam in the ocean and afterwards Hannah sat on the beach, shivering, not wanting to go inside, not wanting to leave the beach, and that night came her fever. It raged and raged and I lifted her, woozy and weak, in the firelight, draping her against me so as to pull off her sweat-drenched clothes. I remember changing the sheets soaked from the fire burning in her, and wrapping her, weak, thin, fragile, shivering, back into bed. Sedna was close, vigilant, her golden eyes serious. Hannah said that Sedna smelled her dreams. She would only leave Hannah long enough to go outside for security sweeps of the perimeter, to snarl at the coyotes she smelled in the night and which she was especially in the mood to kill. A member of the pack was sick. Zero tolerance.

It's raining little drops of darkness, Hannah said. If I ever light all the way on fire just let me burn, she said. She said that she was freezing and to make the fire warmer, to heap the blankets higher, she said I needed to warm her with my body, like Eskimos, she said, and I took off my clothes and lay next to her and her whole body was fire. As she slept and I held her the night grew quieter and the sound of the surf clearer and I thought of the great thing awaiting me. Your son harmed the thing most mine, the principal joy of my world since I was six and thought zebras were magical. How he would bleed.

Hannah's fever fell and two days later, weak and pale and peaceful in the sun on the beach Hannah told me she had made me drive so far for a reason. So that I could understand. She said that I might get confused, that I might not be able to distinguish a wrong done to her from one done to me and so I might try and take what was hers. But you know it's mine, she said. I know you know. That said, you can help. Once you know the rest. Because you only know half of it. I remember how salty the air tasted, the outline of the headlands, the feel of the sand as Hannah told me the rest of her night and I first came to hate you.

I went right to her because I trusted her. That is how Hannah began. She trusted you, the matriarch, to do what must be done. To summon the police in the most dignified manner possible, one that would make her suffer least as they confirmed recent sexual congress with injury. You would know whom to call, how to handle the police, how to direct them to a large, full, ancient house, how to arrest your son and heir and CEO. She said she found you in that most beautiful of all your beautiful rooms, all that wood and stone, and how she told you what happened, the fire crackling loud the whole time, as though surprised, she said, as though angry, and she could see the great tree looming outside, its leaves shivering, everything fast. She saw you believe her, she said. You looked at her kindly, she said, warmly, like family. And you slowed things down.

The alternative before you was clear. Do you sacrifice your grand-daughter to the exceptional situation? Or the exceptional situation to your grand-daughter? Your greatest concern must have been that nothing happen immediately, nothing happen without control, without a plan. Having just prepared the solution to all your problems, the work of years, planning and plotting and arranging and overseeing and waiting, for moving men takes time, you told her about it. You told her the truth, and you told her a story about it, a story about being a matriarch, what it was like and what responsibilities fell to it, given the danger of the seas. You told her of your experience. She heard you say that rape is terrible, as all violence is terrible, that it is especially so in a way that men can never know, you said, for it is an evil of men. You said it mattered greatly, and what came next took her breath away. She heard you tell her that the remediation, as you called it, would need to wait. That it would be no less real for being deferred. That no one, in the interim, not even members of the family, not even her own mother, could know, so important and so delicate was the conjuncture, so imminent the threat, so great the moment, so real the family's need. Women are different from men, you told her, and the more you live the more you see it. Women do not fight like men, they do not run things like men, they do not rule like men and they do not lose their minds like men. Men cannot rule like us, you said, it entails a delicacy they have no way to imagine. When ruling things means running them, accommodating and according and anticipating them, rather than sailing and swinging a broadsword, once it concerns the real work of the world, men are at sea, in the dark, lost.

Looking out at the ocean with Sedna at her side Hannah talked of your voice, how it was broken in a way that showed how much force had been required to break it, how it had a rich warm timbre so that you liked to hear it, hear it say anything: the weather, a ship's log, stock prices, the history of the Syrls. And with that voice you told her what needed to be done, with all that calm reason, with all that knowledge of the world, with all your famous powers of persuasion, you told her what would be, next to that fireplace so huge she could have walked into it, she said. Hannah looked into your eyes, she said, and saw that you had no shame.

Your mistake at this moment was, of course, twofold. The moral mistake is obvious enough. There may be good reasons for killing a person, but none for raping them. Anyone can see that. But not everyone can see the future. You are famous for your foresight. It is what allowed you to bring together all that had been about to happen. And yet you sat across from her and did not see what was before you, did not see that, young as she was, scarcely more than a girl, she was a thousand times more dangerous than Sixten. As the extent of her vengeance shows. Had you consigned your son that night and such a scandal arisen the things you had aligned would doubtless have come apart: offer rejected, merger postponed, engagement cancelled, alliance dissolved, opportunity lost. The information you possessed would soon have lost its incredible value and your family would have continued its course, which was decline. About all this you were doubtless right. And not only did you rightly judge your chances of success, you rightly foresaw a whole series of things Hannah would not do, including whom she would not tell. But the decisive thing you did not see. Not one in a million millions of children is born with such a talent for vengeance, and to that child did you give shelter, warmth, kindness, love? Or did you give her instead a war and a Rome, which she has just burned? Not in the interest of morality or solidarity or justice or being a woman or being her grandmother, but solely in the cool calculation of the Syrls' best interest, you should have offered up your son that night. Did it never occur to you that her unusual mind might be as well suited, or still better, to vengeance as it was to prime numbers and ancient Greek? I wonder if you had any doubts. Because she didn't.

* * *

I have always had a pacific dream life. It is like an inner California where very little happens and the weather is nice and there is one thing that is happening and it is everything. Hannah's was a very different dream-world. Her dreams were like the *Mahabharata*, with dozens of characters and plots and sub-plots and gods and animals and things turning into other things, and never more than in the days after the fever. On the way to school when we were little I found it exhausting just to listen to them. Now, morning after morning, to the sound of the surf and the sight of the Pacific, Hannah told me the dreams in which she saw your end, the design becoming clearer and clearer, and amid all the noise and chaos and deities and demons of those dreams a single outline began to present itself: the one you see now.

Hannah slept differently the first days, very close to me, holding right on to me in sleep, our legs intertwined, like during the Divide. But once she awoke she drifted away. I had to not watch her all the time, she said. I had to let her be. As soon as she caught me looking at her with concern she would flare her nostrils and shake her head and then, in Potawatomi, tell me to move my canoe. More and more often she would call Sedna and sink down on her haunches, strong, like the Ottawa, and Sedna's wolf-bright eyes would narrow and her ears flatten and her hips sway and she would say she was happy, that she was ready, ready to hunt, ready to run, because that is what it is to be a wolf, and what it is to be the daughter of one. One morning when I found Hannah looking into Sedna's strange golden eyes she turned to me and told me that it was not as I thought. I'm quiet, she said, but it's not like you think. I asked her how I thought it was and she told me I knew. I'm not reliving it all over, she said, like a waking nightmare. I'm taking it apart. Carefully. Like a bomb.

From midnight until two every night we went to the rich hippie institute down the road. They opened their redwood gates to the few guests of the Norwegian as part of an ancient agreement concerning land. Or water. The condition for entrance was complete silence, as the night baths were silent for all, guests and visitors. We walked the huge sloping moonlit lawn down to the cliff and the pools carved from its black rock. The smell of the springs was sharp and sedative. They overlooked the ocean to such an extent that they were literally unsafe. The first night when Hannah reached farther and farther out over the edge, her body poised above nothing, the Pacific crashing below, I had a bad thought and grabbed her ankle, although there was no need, no risk of that, as you saw.

Surfing, swimming, water, sand, sun, dog, fire, night, repeat, day after day, night after night. One day after she raked her leg across the reef I saw the plume of bright blood, felt fear, but she was fine, it was only blood, she said, and she watched the gentle insistence with which Sedna licked her cuts clean. Don't worry, she said. I'm bleeding to get stronger. That's how we do it.

Most nights I'd wake and find Hannah outside, with Sedna, watching the waves, watching the woods, watching the night. One night she slept until morning. And then a few nights later she did it again until, hour by hour, she reclaimed her rest. In the meantime she read, more than ever. All day, all night, at the breakfast table, on the porch with her father's peacoat wrapped round her, at the beach, before the fire, in bed, day after day, night after night, reading.

The Wise One visited bearing, as ever, books. Hannah loved reading his books, their margins filled with minute penciling, his mind so full of surprises. The books were all about ancient Rome. They had covers of red cloth and they spoke not of the founding of Rome, not of the twins or the wolf or the hills or the Senate or the aqueducts or the emperors or Cleopatra or the Coliseum but only of one thing: Hannibal of Carthage. For the Wise One was wise. He saw things still far away, storm clouds in her skies, the way she was turning, and so he tried to change the weather.

At first Hannah talked about what had happened, when she talked about it, in mythic terms. That was how the Wise One had taught us to view extreme situations. They tried to Iphigenia me, she said, looking out at the ocean. For wind. I will show them wind, she said. I will show them Iphigenia. Another day it was Sedna. Her Sedna would tell her many animals, her many children, the dolphins, the walruses, the blue whales and grey whales and killer whales to turn on the village, and that when they went to sea, the entire village, as they did each year to give themselves to the waters from which they came, she would send her animals against them, and smash their boats and drown them and pull them down to the seafloor, to the place where they told her to live. But with the red books all that changed.

Rome and Carthage were both old, Hannah said. Both cities were powerful, both rising. And with all the world watching they went to war. Spectators all around the Mediterranean—in Egypt, in Judea, in Greece, in Sicily, in Spain—were unable to take their eyes off it or say who would win. The Carthaginians ruled the waves. But they had a normal taste for fighting and no more. The Romans had a remarkable taste for it, into it passed all their civic pride. They did not fight in wild, dangerous, doomed conflict like

Gauls or Germans. They fought like professionals and it was terrifying to go into battle against them because, Hannah said, they were quiet. They weren't screaming and shouting, they didn't need to yell courage into themselves. They were going to work, killing you.

The Carthaginians were not like that. They were merchants. They lived on the sea, and the greatest conflict for them was with the sea, with its storms and submerged currents and flow of fortune. After a crushing naval loss Carthage surrendered rather than risk having its city, older, richer, more beautiful than Rome, plundered, its wives and daughters raped, its temples pillaged, its city sacked. So much stronger at sea, or believing themselves to be, and yet losing at sea, stirred superstitions and many saw it as a sign from the gods to sue for peace, to get a good price for it, which they did. In guarantee for good behavior Carthage had to give Rome her sons. All of them. The Romans were good at hostages, Hannah said. The sons of Carthage did not languish in prisons. Something far more terrible was done with them. They were made Roman. Every Carthaginian senator had to send his sons to Rome, to be raised with every comfort, tutored by the wisest men, doing as they liked, as free and privileged as any boy from a great Roman family. The result was that they would grow foreign to their home. That was how Rome operated, said the Wise One. It would leave rich Carthage intact, but deprived of heirs, and thus of her means of vengeance. But, Hannah said, they missed one.

Every day on the beach Hannah told me more. Unlike every other Carthaginian general, Hamilcar Barca never lost a battle to the Romans during the first war with Rome. He never lost one ever. He never even drew. And yet his city lost the war, sued for peace, bent to Rome. So he went with his army deep into Spanish territory Rome did not hold and took his small, bright-eyed, fast-minded son with him. When the boy was still small he was led by moonlight to a high cliff overlooking the sea, with Rome in the distance, invisible, but there, and the boy swore an oath. The goddess of fire was real to Hannibal, she was what burned in fire, what made fire move as it did and do what it could. But he swore his oath less to the goddess than to his father, Hannah said, the sea at their feet, the fire flickering before them, and in the oath was his whole life, so that when his father died there was only one fire left to start, in Rome. He swore to make Rome bend, to take it, and when it was taken go to the temple of the Vestals with their sacred fire burning for six centuries and blow it right fucking out.

Night and day, beach and house, sand and fire, Hannah read and spoke of war. It flowed from her. She talked about it when we lay on the beach, when we walked Sedna, when we were in bed, when we drove, even when we swam. She told me of the silver mines and the wars with the Spanish tribes. Hannibal was like no other boy. From an early age he could do things no one else could. He was already a complete soldier in training, vision and even authority as an adolescent. He was made for war. It fit his genius. And everyone around him saw this so clearly that they followed him, with pride and fascination, for if there were gods they clearly loved him. How else do you do what he does, and how else does one get an army to march across three Roman provinces, ford a deadly river, then climb over the Alps, with winter coming, at a pass so treacherous the Romans didn't guard it, with elephants? She told me that the farmers in Italy, in the valley of the Po, stared to see, with the coming of the first snows, an African army descend, tall black men on horseback, Spaniards in leather, Gauls of the long swords, a great army, its elephants festooned for war, bound for Rome. And no sooner was young Hannibal in Italy than he marched into battle and got to see what happened when his mind really lit on fire, when he saw that it had always been on fire, with as result three successive battles with Rome, the three worst, most overwhelming, most humiliating, most annihilating military defeats in a thousand years of Roman history. He cut them down like nothing, saw through them like glass, tore through them like a bull, she said. And as her eyes looked into the fire, looked out to sea, looked down at the dust, I saw what the Wise One had done.

In book after book she read of Hannibal. Everything she could find. Historical studies, archaeology bulletins, academic articles, things about coins, Spanish novels based on his life which she said were terrible but good. When the Wise One returned he addressed the issue. The people of history are interesting, he said, how could they not be, given that time has effaced everything but the outline of action. But you, my girl, have missed the outline. You are in a remarkable situation. So you think of remarkable things. You might be a Barca, he said, you might be a Hannibal. I have always found you exceptional and have never made a secret of it. But look what happens to genius, look what happens to Hannibal. He was the greatest military genius of which there has ever been any record. He marched elephants over the Alps when barely more than a boy and for a decade and a half no army could defeat him, even when he was ridiculously outnumbered. Each battle was more devastating and more brilliant than the last for the simple reason that he always intuited more about his opponents than they could imagine. Each time the Romans thought they had understood something about his mind and his army, they were right, they had. But in the time it took he had learned many times more and so each time they went back into the field against him, each time the glory of Rome with its purple and its eagles marched out to meet him, he did not just defeat them, he destroyed them, each time more outnumbered, each time more devastating, each time on Roman territory, year after year.

The Wise One was nervous and paced the Norwegian's deck. He asked Hannah if she recalled Cannae. Her eyes glowed yes. At Cannae, Hannibal was outnumbered more than two to one, she said. And yet it wasn't even close. Of the 90,000 Romans something on the order of 5,000 were able to flee. All the rest were killed or captured. And this hadn't been some random group of 90,000 people. It had been 90,000 Roman soldiers, otherwise known as the terror of the civilized world. Hannibal did that.

Which is the point of the story, the Wise One said, the outline of action. Cannae did not give Hannibal Rome. Not even the perfect victory gave him that. And in the end he did not win his war because Rome was just too many and too patient. And the Syrls, child, are too many and too patient. Even if you are patient, even if you are perfect, even if you are as great as Hannibal of Carthage they will always be too many. And would you not agree that it is childish to march elephants over the Alps and fight outnumbered for years killing Romans and never defeating Rome, never taking Rome, never burning Rome? Would it not be better to live peacefully, happily, in Spain?

Hannah's face had the sun on it, more freckled than ever. She was quiet a long time, her eyes far, on the water, breathing, gathering, and at last she straightened and told your brother, I see that, I see Spain. But as much as if my father had lit a fire and sacrificed a white ram and touched blood to blood, I am bound. Then she told the Wise One of the very end of her night.

Before I left that house that night, she said, before I disappeared in the night, I went to the tree. I drove there, she said, in someone's car, across the lawns. She said that when she was a baby her father sat with her under the tree and so she'd known it longer than she could remember. I left the car far away so as not to invade the tree's space and walked barefoot across the cold grass, slick with dew, farther and farther from the house, the night larger, the forest breathing out cool air, and there it was, alone, on its hill, and I lay down under the tree stretching above me in the night and I listened. She asked the Wise One if he remembered the oracle. After my father's funeral you had told me a story about a tree, she said. You walked with me and wanted to distract me, thought it would be good to distract me because you thought that I might hurt myself with the memory of him, so you started talking, telling me that Greek oracles were showy affairs. Marble colonnades winding their way up the mountain, statues every step of the way, and at the top a cave, dark, filled with strange odors, and a beautiful woman speaking an unearthly tongue, raving, swaying, and before you could begin to understand a eunuch escorted you out, telling you what you had just heard, what had just happened, and thus whether you should attack Corinth, or rather not. But they had not always been showy, the first oracle was simple, it was like our tree, you said. A huge, mighty, ancient oak, struck by lightning and thus sacred to the Thunderer. In the rustle of its leaves the priests of the oracle heard the future. You told me that the priests lived in constant contact with the tree, walking around it during the day, sleeping beneath it at night, so I lay down and I listened to my family tree for a long time, she said. I considered burning the whole house down that night. Then I realized that wouldn't do. Not by half, she said.

A few days later I awoke to a note smearily written with eyeliner pencil. I lifted it off the pillow and read: SILVER MINES! I wandered outside, wrapped in a blanket, and found fog. The surfers at the first break were only visible when they caught waves, the rest of the world shrouded so I fell back to sleep on the porch, listening to the surf. Sedna arrived, followed by Hannah, wet, shivery, awake from the ocean.

You got my note, she said, wiping eyeliner off my cheek. You found silver, I said. I found silver, she confirmed. Excited, out of breath, pulling off her wetsuit, she told me that elephants were not free.

Iberian rock-slingers who can hit a man on horseback at a hundred yards were not free. Libyan infantry. Numidian cavalry. Greeks. Gauls. None of them free. And as the sun burned away the fog and the day caught up with itself Hannah told me of her plan. After the end of the first Punic war, Hamilcar Barca asked for money from Carthage so as to raise a new army in Spain, beyond Roman reach. Carthage did not reply, and so, being the sort of person he was, he made his own money. He found silver, mined it, minted it, and used it to form an army, used it to get ready for war. It takes money to take money, Hannah said, removing her Canadian sunglasses. So I need a silver mine. And one has just become available.

Even if you had not disinherited your youngest son he would never have touched your money. It was not in his nature. Your offer to trade her harm for cash, to let her inherit all her father would have, to return her to the list of legitimate heirs was, as she said, a golden leash. I won't be able to use much of it, she said, not for what I want to use it for. Giving her money was the best way to control her, to track her movements, to encourage addiction. And to accept it, she said, was the best way to begin blinding you.

While I slept, Hannah had talked to Justin and learned of the arrest of the only credible drug dealer in our school, a senior who had already turned 18 and was thus in the deepest trouble. Marijuana circulated freely through all local educational institutions, but it did so in very random strains, whereas if you wanted serious drugs there was only him, and serious drugs meant high quality marijuana and cocaine and whichever of the pills happened to be easiest to obtain at that moment in the year's drug calendar. At the moment of his arrest this included oxy. He's definitively fucked, she said. Even if he gets out of it his family will screw him so deeply in place he'll never move again. But nature doesn't care, she said, nature abhors a vacuum.

I said I wasn't selling oxy. I had taken it once, with Hannah, having subluxated my sacro-iliac in a soccer game, tackled by Justin. When the hospital released me they gave me two pills. I took one and gave the other to her. It was magical. I could feel all that was bruised, all that was torn, all that was hurt, but it did not frighten or even frustrate me. It was just there, it would get better, everything would. It was one of the most enjoyable nights of my life. We walked the dogs, watched a high-school hockey game, mesmerized, went to a pizzeria with a view of a cemetery, none of which is likely to sound very magical unless you are, at this moment, taking a synthetic opiate, which given your age is not to be ruled out, but also not to be relied upon. I found it amazing but I was not about to start selling it. I don't see silver, I said, and Hannah told me it was because I got up too late. He got caught with pills and coke, she said, so he gave the police his pill supplier and his coke supplier. But he was out of weed. *Nada*. So he didn't have to roll on Arturo's cousins. Which is a good thing because that would be a terrible idea. Our school is the silver mine? I asked. One of them, she said. The other one we have to dig. On university property.

I think they show great restraint, Hannah said of Arturo's cousins, especially given the shit they have to hear. Look at it from their perspective. The whole country, even California, is constantly telling them to fuck off back to wherever their grandparents were born, which is usually some place that was totally green and beautiful before we arrived and is now hell on earth. Think how it must look to them. All of these lunatic white people who hate them for no reason—people whose ancestors, it should be remembered, murdered the people who lived here before, blankets with smallpox, women and children and babies, full-on genocide, which means they are dealing with people who have an attested history of genocidal murder. And to make matters scarier they are protected by a lunatic fringe of very violent cops. That they try to change the given is normal and healthy and human. But they can't afford to sell around town. Not like us.

Hannah took with her everywhere she went a relic of the Old One, an old French map of the Great Lakes. There was the well-drawn east coast, the only part the mapmaker had really nailed. There was the Mississippi. There were huge blank spaces to the west. And there was the Nation of Fire. Michigan wasn't a mitten on the map. It looked like a badly made arrowhead. The satellite image of Michigan looks, of course, just like a mitten, but the old mapmakers didn't want to get accused of simplified drawing, said the Old One, so they made a bad arrowhead. Hannah took a sheet of paper and copied the map, then began tracing long lines across it. She drew a line moving from the Mississippi to Chicago, from Chicago to Detroit to Toronto, a line that passed through our town. The supply line is there, she said, it just needs to make a stop. Off the west coast of Michigan, in the waters of Lake Michigan, Hannah made the calculations for a quarter ounce, a half-ounce, an ounce, a pound. Like the Old One, she said, we will trade on the Great Lakes and our canoe will grow heavy with silver.

Her pitch to Arturo's cousins was short, in Spanish, and surprising. All the more as her Spanish was theirs. A plant that grows freely, all over the world, with a huge variety of medicinal and social benefits, has a natural value, she told Arturo's cousins. And yet, for various political reasons, like needing a pretext to hassle Latinos, it is placed in a category alongside substances made of chemical fertilizer which make everyone who takes them lose their minds, like crystal meth, literal poison. But this, she said, is not our defense if we get caught, our defense is that it was not us, that we had nothing to do with it, that those are not ours, that they are all lies and corruption and confusion and we are children, we are minors and demand our parents and their imperious lawyers, now. That, she said, is what happens if they find us with the wrong backpack. Think about our parents, she said. She turned to Arturo, who had been going to school with us since second grade. She recalled the life of her father, often arrested, often protesting. She noted that my parents had lived in Quebec, in northern California, were obviously 420 forever. If we get caught they will not be on any side but ours, she said, and they will put no pressure on us to roll. As is on clear display in the world's great criminal organizations, the best way to engage in illegal activity is by doing so exclusively with family and those one has known since childhood. Arturo has known us as children, he knows the shape of our character. Then Hannah turned to practical matters.

The high school market is right there, ready, waiting, she said. But there is another. The college market is too large not to have holes, holes you can't fill, holes to dig, mines. What do college kids at a large public university with low admission requirements and an intense sporting culture want? To party, she said. What do they need for this? Drugs. They have money, which they are unused to and thus use unwisely. One of our classmates, someone who had gone to preschool with us, had an older brother who had just entered a fraternity, was on the college soccer team, had a six-foot boa constrictor and had been struck by lightning. He had survived because at the moment of illumination he was running and only his right foot was touching the ground, the bolt grounding through the right side of his body, missing his heart by very little. He is destined for notoriety, Hannah said, and the kids in the fraternity will count on him to have local drug connections. We have an understanding.

In every college town there is an ancestral knowledge of how to profit from students. It is like having an army pass through your area. Or caribou. It can be profitable, but they trample your fields. We had grown up learning to avoid college kids in general and fraternity members in particular. They were morally indefensible, they were the enemy in training, and exactly, Hannah said, the people to acquire large quantities of drugs. And yet they have fears, she said. They are scared of arrest, incarceration, robbery, violence, injury, and humiliation. Whom do they associate with these things? Minorities. Whom do they not associate with them? White kids from the local gifted high school. We will give them the sense they are getting over on us, and thereby get over on them. No matter how much we get caught with or how threatening the cops, your name we never breathe. We do not want you to have the slightest reason to be upset with us. We know you can roll us whenever you like, she said. We're not playing that kind of game. We're not playing a game at all. We're doing business with businessmen, we're behaving honorably to honorable people. We are making a deal.

We were reliable, efficient, intrepid, and charged a huge markup. The skaters reported back to Arturo that we, in fact, never mentioned his name or those of his cousins. We heard rumors filter back to us that our weed came from Chicago, Toronto, Detroit, California. That it was from Algonquin Park, from Ann Arbor, that it was grown on a hippie farm in the Upper Peninsula, in a secret greenhouse, in a hidden bunker. Hannah once told a gym class, in Arturo's presence, that the growers were activist friends of my mother's in northern California, from the lost coast, from the Eden of weed. She said that weed grew best there for reasons of a more or less sacred nature, and that they sent the weed to us in a bear canister. The delivery services use dogs, she said, thus the bear canisters. She told them if you go camping in California, in the Upper Peninsula, in Canada, in the lands of the Old One, and you just fall asleep with food in your tent a bear will come and wake you up and that will be the end. People up there put everything, even wrappers, she said, in bear canisters. So the Californians drive up to where there are bears and buy a bear canister, and they ask to have it left in its original packaging, for invoicing purposes, for their lodge, which doesn't exist. Then they carefully open the package, fill the canister with premium weed, and not only seal it so the dogs can't smell it, they put it back in the original packaging so that the postal service treats it as commercial shipping. And then they send it by ground transport so that it never passes through an airport, and very slowly the postal service brings it to your door—or, in this case, to a place where they actually might use a bear canister, the Old One's cabin. Other stories were invented on other occasions, protecting the location of the mine being, as Hannah observed, the first rule of mining.

Deliveries were, of necessity, risky. Fraternity parties, which in the past we visited as one would a safari, were now operational ventures comporting risk. Here Justin excelled. We used the punk rock kids playing shows in Chicago, Ann Arbor, Detroit, Toronto, to make connections, but decided they shouldn't transport. Cops didn't like punks. Preppy kids should transport, and be paid handsomely for it. They should look young and innocent. Preferably with golf bags in the trunk. Real worst of the worst, Hannah said. The skater kids were extremely well rewarded. College kids asked them for weed all the time anyway. Their level of information was very high and their willingness to speak with the police very low. They were always moving around, always outside, always watching, and people had trouble distinguishing them. We made a long list of kids, from the philosophy club, from the soccer team, rich kids, and in the waters of Lake Huron noted their future functions. Skaters and hippie kids could do the small street dealing on the frontier where town and university met. We drew up a jock list that would deal to the fraternities. We noted the people who worked in the bars and pizzerias and the taquerias. Absentee-ish parents whose houses could be used. Hannah's own house. My mother's. My father's. The Old One's cottage, which he had left to Gaby and me, was the main depot. We were careful to stress that there was a huge bonus for not snitching if caught, and reminded all that as minors they wouldn't get in real trouble, unless they were black or Hispanic, and no matter their parents we kept them out, our racist cops were always watching those kids in a way that was perfectly obvious, terrible, and contrary to our purposes.

Had you asked smugglers to design a school for their purposes they might have made ours. It was the opposite of a panopticon. You couldn't see anything from anywhere, the forest growing right up against and around it. We enlisted unusual talents. Jimmy Edmunds had logged the most spectacular failure the regional rehab people had ever seen, testing positive for, in the director's words, a Mexican pharmacy of illicit substances. We saw the official email, for he had hacked his parents' accounts and conducted extensive correspondence on their behalf. He forwarded the list of substances in his system, a few of which he admitted to taking just to raise the count. More importantly, his general mood was itself an advertisement for drug use. Going undercover at that age is easy, adolescents being so mutable that no one is surprised when their look changes. Hannah suggested a change and Jimmy stopped dressing like a punk and started dressing like, in her words, Little Lord Fauntleroy. Out with the Crucifucks t-shirts, in with Polo, on with the uniform of obedience. We thought he went too far. Too far is the whole point, he maintained. I want to look like my parents won. And to police this says I am the child of the mean ones, the ones you serve and protect. It's not that they need to think I'm innocent. It is that they need to think I'm not worth it. That if you hassle me my parents are only too willing to become total nightmares, ones they can't make go away just by kicking someone's ass.

We were a fair trade organization, reflected by our happy reign and significant warchest. The rewards we gave were lavish, the punishments few and, where Justin was involved, exemplary. We allowed for online payment, and started to put most of the silver in bitcoin. You may see the principal heredity of your banking family in Hannah's instinct not to have all her money in the same place, or even in the same kind of place. Drachmas and lire are gone, she said, now there is this stuff. I wasn't a fan of bitcoin, suspicious it might disappear into the darkness of the deep web. I was wrong.

The close of business came in a decrepit abbey in downtown Detroit, close to the river, close to the border, smelling no longer of incense or prayer but of beer and mildew and sweat. We found Jimmy in the balcony, under a table, watching the show. He had taken some cocktail of drugs that made standing, but not enjoyment, impossible. He had a trusting relationship with drugs, like someone who handled venomous snakes. He remained calm. And he told us what he had heard, told us that they were coming, told us of the end.

Without wanting to, without meaning to, we had begun to emit a constant signal, to show up on a certain radar. You may imagine how easy it is to get into trouble with professional drug dealers. They are, of course, phenomenally territorial. And they must create a universe in which opposing them is something only an insane person would do, something even a junkie would think twice about doing. That so many gangsters who smoke lots of weed end up shooting people attests to how incredibly stressful a job it is. Good drug dealers are very intuitive about what they can do to and with you, so they check you out when they meet you in a uniquely intense way. Those they sent were scary. Tattoos on the face scary. But nothing was half so scary as the eyes of the messenger, flickering between hate and indifference, like sun through leaves. The huge advantage of excessive violence was presented to us. It said do not mess, do not cross, do not lie, do not wrong and if I ask for something, even something excessive, give it to me, for you have only this life.

That night, shivering on the shore of the Detroit River we saw the future. You can smell Canada from here, Hannah said. Accept and move. So we made an offering, told a lie, and disappeared in the night, marching for Rome, ready at last for you.

When Hannah first surfed the Norwegian's break an old Californian stopped to watch. He asked her when she had learned to surf it, then he saw from her hesitation that she had never surfed it before, that what he had seen were her first waves. The Elders watched her all morning and when she came in, pulling off her wetsuit, they gestured her over for what she thought would be some routine sexual harassment and which was, instead, their blessing. Then they told her the thing she had come for. They told her the weather underground.

That night on the porch, waiting for a storm to roll in, smelling the sea, watching the waves grow, hearing them grow, the pound of them louder and louder, Hannah spoke. Her father's peacoat wrapped around her honey-colored legs, she told Sedna of her plan. Hannah often talked to dogs, hers and others, Sedna most of all. I had fallen asleep on the porch, waiting for the storm, and when I woke it had come, big, white, crashing surf in the darkness, and Hannah's back was to me, her eyes were on it, were in the ocean, her fingers moving through Sedna's thick wolfy fur, gentle on Sedna's pregnant belly. She told Sedna it was dangerous to surf in the dark and that she wanted to. She told her that people who live next to the ocean have a different rhythm, its rhythm. She said that while surfing may be a strange activity to people who live even a few miles inland, for those who grow up next to the ocean it is the most natural thing in the world. She told Sedna that there were even dogs that could do it. And then as I was slipping back to sleep she told Sedna what she was preparing for you.

I'm killing a bad alpha, Hannah said. Once there was a pack of wolves in Canada and men came and shot the males. Females in a pack do not go into heat at the same time, she informed Sedna, except in extraordinary circumstances, like this one. There were two sisters, she said, in the same pack. The eldest was the alpha. Bad. She told Sedna that aggression is a function of fear. The bad alpha was frightened in some deep part of her and so she ruled her pack with cruelty, with aggression, always snarling and biting and humiliating. She could not lead otherwise than by aggression, she did not know how, so she made every member of the pack uneasy, made them tense, and stress is bad for the wolf. The bad alpha had her pups first. And as soon as she was strong enough she followed the scent of her sister, the scent of her sister's pups, to kill them. Being a mother, Hannah said, is special, becoming a mother is to become strong, it has a special force and a special fury. A mother, she said, is a dangerous thing. Hannah told Sedna how Alaska bared her fangs the night she was born. Akna is the Inuit goddess of birth, Hannah said, and her name means strength. So when the bad alpha came to kill her little sister's pups she found the younger wolf outside the den, weak from giving birth, strong from being a mother, eyes glowing, head high, and she who had always submitted to her sister did not submit. She fought the bad alpha, fought her huge sister, to death. Then she went to her sister's den and took her bad alpha pups in her mouth and carried them one after another to her own den, fed them from her body, raised them with her own, and when they came of age they formed the strongest pack the valley had ever seen. It is important to fight bad alphas, Hannah said. It's a responsibility. Then Hannah stood up and they ran down the long stretch of dark sand to the water, and dove in.

The answer to your lawyers' question about surveillance is that of course Hannah had access to bank and personal communications, yours, Sixten's, others. She had access to the most varied communications, and could not have had it otherwise, given what she was going to do. It began with the first bright bits of silver, the first funds in bitcoin, as Hannah commissioned a report on you, then another, and another, and another. She couldn't simply see your vulnerabilities with the naked eye. They were not posted online. So we went into the dark of the web and hired different kinds of searchers to do different kinds of searching. A school like ours encouraged both a high degree of computer literacy and an eagerness to misuse it. But it was through Arturo's cousins that she learned about the most important things for sale on the dark web. Hannah's fingers fast on the keyboard, happy, running, hunting, shopping. It's like Ikea, she said, scrolling through the malware, and soon she was spending large amounts in the pure currency of the internet, coin of the realm, so as to have a look around your domains. It did not take long for her to see the decision tree, or you in it. And it did not take her long to see the shape of her opportunity, to see the height of your Alps and the way across them. The greatest risk was always you, would always be you, she said. After all, had you realized an hour earlier everything would have been different. And had you realized a week earlier nothing would have happened at all. So from the first her plan grew to your measure, needing always and above all to seem like no plan at all. For a time. But the goal was never that it remain a secret forever, only that it do so long enough to complete your fall. Then you could see. The 'Ndrangheta would have shot you one in front of the other until the oldest, the deepest living root of the tree, had watched all those of his line die at his feet. Hannah planned to do something more refined, but in the same spirit.

There was one type of information Hannibal of Carthage wanted above all others, she said, information about the character of the general opposing him. Was he impulsive, cautious, eager for fame, frightened of his position? How was he when drunk, how did he treat women, was he physically brave? These are all important questions when the game is to think like the other. Although Hannah learned to see through you, and thus to predict your movements, this required a great deal of minute study, given your strength, given your tusks. Getting access to your files, your computers, your accounts, emails, messages, was the first priority, the first item on her list. Thereafter, anything you seemed to notice, anything you seemed to suspect was discontinued, discarded, transformed into the innocuous. That was the rule. The night she told him of her plan, the Wise One asked if she heard under the family tree how she was to uproot it. Did you hear under the tree how you were to do it? he asked. Is it accessible to reason? The Wise One paced the deck, cursing the Norwegian. He was agitated. Of course it is accessible to reason, Hannah replied. It's a plan. Would you like to hear it? He gestured with impatient wisdom for her to begin.

You taught us that everything is fire, everything fast, mobile, consuming. And you taught us that everything is water, upon which they sail. You taught us that rare is the person born in this world who is not, sooner or later, appalled by it, rare the person who finds herself in the juggernaut and says, this is perfect, this is Eden, this is exactly what one would think, no surprises here. You say I have no allies, she said, but that is not so. The Syrls make clear that if others must suffer so that their wines may be fine beyond compare, so be it. The Syrls say, I support the iniquitous order of the world because it is not iniquitous to me. Which means I have all the allies I could ever need. Nothing lives that long without acquiring enemies. And now a bank makes enemies simply by being a bank. Think of all the places where they are violent, where the Syrls bring violence, violence in the form of rubber production, violence in the form of logging concerns, violence in the form of mineral extraction, violence in the form of satellites, violence in the form of children drinking filthy water and men with their teeth kicked in for minding. Violence breeds hate, she said, everyone knows that. The people who ran Enron were obviously scumbags, but they were unknown, unreal, and, moreover, already caught and punished. Whereas the Syrls were none of these things. The Syrls were ready for sacrifice.

With a stick in the sand of the Californian beach Hannah drew the blueprint for your blackout. She traced her route through Spain and over the Pyrenees, across the Rhone, over the Alps, and down into the fertile valleys of Italy where she would undo you. Her first idea had been publicity, exposure, Calumny, as she called it. But every time she played out the scenarios, every time she imagined what might happen, every time she ran the numbers, they were too low. As she lay shivering beneath your family tree, as she sat on the beach watching the waves, as she looked into the fire, as she surfed, as she ate, slept, fucked, she imagined the possibilities of publicity, of things hidden which might be found, recordings, revelations, leaks, stories, feeds, infamy, calumny. And each time she saw the limit, saw that it would always be possible to say that the girl was lying and the world, knowing that some girls lie, would go about its business, given your business. It would not suffice for total interruption of service, for the complete vilification and destitution of your family, the loss of its political position, its connections to the crown, not suffice for the public damning of its name. So there had to be more, much more.

Hannah knew from her father how your wealth was old, how the roots of it had grown deep and ramified wide. You were raised in wealth such that it seemed you would never be parted from it, like a castle on so steep a cliff, over so treacherous a fjord, that anyone who looked would see that it was time to leave. And yet money wouldn't be money if there were not some way of taking it away, she said, even if guarded by dragons. The Wise One taught us that Odysseus won the war through the effects of the war.

All the Greeks had achieved after a decade of siege, a decade of war, a decade of Achilles killing every warrior who went outside the high walls to face him was to make all Trojans deeply share one thing: hatred of the Greeks. Only Odysseus saw the advantage this represented, the way they thirsted for vengeance, the way they missed their life of riding and ruling those plains, the way they wanted not just to survive the siege, but to win it. So he married their love to their hate. They loved nothing so much as horses, hated nothing so much as Greeks, so much so that when they saw the Gift they would burn to have it. I have something similar in mind, she said. I am going to build for the Syrls a beautiful Horse, like Odysseus, and fuck them with it.

Despite having read a huge amount of your email, despite sifting through your activities for more hours than I can count, I don't know whether you know why your youngest son did as he did, why your wealth so appalled him. Whether you know its cause or not, you will have surmised that your youngest son did not teach Hannah that wealth insures life, that wealth is a good in itself, that being born wealthy is a supreme good. He told her to be as careful with wealth as with the Japanese knives in the kitchen. Extreme wealth is incredibly sharp, he said. It divides everything, and many never learn how to handle it, never learn how to keep it separate from the love in their lives, and so they cut themselves and others with it again and again until they are all scarred. Who has so very much money? he asked. And why? So that those of their line, of their house, of their blood will always be beyond the reach of the world? That's supposed to be good for them? There are always nicer things, he told his only daughter, faster cars and larger houses, but it will all bore you unless you live only for toys, unless you live as a child. And so before his death your youngest told Hannah that many others thought as he did, that there was weather underground, and he told her, should she ever need to, how to find it.

Your son's former allies told Hannah what she wanted to know, but could only tell so much, could tell who but not how, where but not when, could tell of the existence of the Institute, but not its location. So she tore down her wall and went to Annika and asked for her help. Not in return for anything. When Hannah finally told her the full extent of what she was going to do, she said she was scared that Annika would make her stop, would tell you, but her cousin just beamed, and for the first time in their lives they were close. Annika's desire to destroy you may have been childish, may have been insane, but then again you do not choose your family, and you go to war with the soldiers you have.

Your lawyers ask how we entered into contact with officials of your bank. They ask how we came to know the Institute of Measurement and Control. Annika said that people wildly underestimate the information that moves through the night. Because they need to, she said. Most people cannot live with what they do. A city of banking dimensions, one the size of New York, Stockholm, London, makes a great deal of noise in the night, if you know how to listen, and presents a great deal of vulnerability, if you can see in the dark. The later it gets the less those in a club, at a party, breathing in the night air, recall where the lines run, and they so love the feeling of not caring that they literally cannot get enough. Through this space Annika moved. And the next morning, when the light returns, when the sun rises, when in the first moments upon awakening in a strange place with strange people and a strange taste in the mouth they feel a wave of worry and shiver of suspicion, they wonder whether they need to feel fear, whether they have just broken a golden rule, there is Annika to assure them all is fine, nothing happened, nothing said, nothing heard, nothing doing. Discontinuous memory is scary for an addled mind, Annika told us, and so they tell themselves that if they broke a rule it could not have been golden. Drifting through the bars and the clubs, the hotel rooms and the homes, around the pools and out on the balconies, like smoke, like a dream, Annika went searching for what Hannah needed, searching casually, so casually that it was dismissed as her just being her, as being her way, and who could change that?

Then, one day, one night, Annika sailed, unawares, into the waters of the Institute of Measurement and Control. The Weather had given Hannah a bit of intelligence, that two of its members were new, that they particularly liked the money of Measurement, that they were said to be out most nights, somewhere. They're coders who have just discovered the real world, there's no time to lose, Hannah said, and so she and Annika got right to work.

Hannah's first business meeting with Measurement took place in front of the Virgin of the Rocks, early afternoon, sobriety and propriety and a class of eight-year-olds in the next room. The Envoy said that every square foot of London was filmed and asked if that felt right. He asked her to have the kindness of not looking at him, and as he attended to the angle of his hood she looked into the painting, relaxing her mind into it, setting the scene she wanted.

What do you need to know? he asked quietly.

The possibilities for perversion of system, she said.

What system? he asked, and when she said your name she said she could feel his body lift, straighten, tense, ready. There was no way to rob the Syrls of their wealth, he said. None at all. I don't want to rob them, she said, I want to ruin them. That's different. That is different, the Envoy acknowledged. And as her mind moved around the Virgin, the rocks, the sign given, the sign received, she sought to move him. The old Weathermen had told her who and what had made Measurement, had told her its guiding notion, and she reminded the Envoy of this. All you say may be true, the Envoy said, but why should we expend all those resources on the Syrls? The bad you say is as true of another bank as of theirs. Maybe, Hannah said. But that's not the point. Everything has a beginning, pointing her finger toward the painting. Surely the overthrow of an iniquitous order has to start somewhere. A first grotto, a first domino, a first head has to fall somewhere. And I have a remarkable grotto and a remarkable head for you. If you are as measured and as controlled as I hear then we can do more than ruin a single bad bank. We can teach the whole watching world how to do it themselves. Which is what you want, said Hannah. So don't be shy about it.

* * *

Every once in a while a bright child is shown the world and says, no, not on those terms, no way. Annika used something she called forensic dancing to discover exactly how Measurement began, to learn of the bright child who said no. She heard that while studying mathematics at Berkeley the first Controller helped a small company with simple programming, coding, answering email, a few hours a week, for years, and when his employers didn't have enough money they paid him in shares, which weren't worth anything, but they had become friends, and it was only money. And then one morning with the birds singing like any other, he awoke to staggering wealth, for it so happens that if A is swallowed by B and B swallowed by C then all the little a's are given an absurd amount of money. Or at least he was.

With his shocking wealth he created a punk rock slush fund to keep small labels afloat, all donations anonymous. It is like taking oil-coated seabirds and cleaning them by hand, Annika was told. Very labor-intensive. And they don't like being touched. He made donations to Oxfam in the names of all the great Montreal Canadiens hockey players. And when he found that was not enough for his heart he founded the Institute of Measurement and Control, with its small brass plaque and its official registration as an internet security firm licensed to possess the very proprietary programs necessary for the Wreckoning he began to prepare.

For the Institute of Measurement and Control a terrible thing is underway, so vast that few see its outline, so bright that few see the look in its eye. The plunder and ruin of the richest communicative resource since the invention of language was not, however, going to happen on their watch, they wouldn't have that on their conscience when they passed into the nihilist afterdeath. When Hannah asked the Envoy why all don't see it, he was quiet an instant and asked, How could they? From most points it is invisible, the space is shaped that way, that is its curvature, that is the respect in which it is evil. But if you see the society from our angle then it is perfectly clear that everything is as it is so as to conceal changeability. It is the entire point of power to appear as fixed in place as a giant stone, to appear given. And yet with the right measurement, the right control, the right institute, he said, anything can be moved.

Hannah needed people who had your downfall at heart for many reasons, one of which was that notwithstanding the silver from the mines, notwithstanding the inheritance you returned to her, notwithstanding her not inconsiderable powers of persuasion, she needed a huge discount. The time of people who can hack into the temperature settings of a nuclear reactor is very expensive. As you might imagine. After a plenary meeting the Institute of Measurement and Control offered its extensive resources *pro bono*. Or *malo*, depending on your perspective. If it is any consolation, they said you were close to having a closed circuit of unbreakable encryption. Your rings of fire were very impressive, they said. To move onto the system what we did, we would not just need a guard to look the other way, they said, we would need a whole regiment to do so. They told us to imagine it like a vapor trail in the sky, very visible, briefly. Which meant that we needed to keep your eyes fixed on the ground, and the best way to do that, they said, has always been to light the ground on fire. Hannah worked with Measurement to make for you a special something, what they called a hornet's nest, then another, and another, and another. Viruses, malware, Furies, Hannah called them, sent screaming through your system, darkening whole areas of functionality, interrupting lines of communication, so that millions of pre-programmed disastrous decisions might be made in your name in less time than you could imagine. The Envoy told the Virgin of the Rocks that lots of the code through which programs run has inefficiencies, redoubling, which is not removed because stopping flow even for an instant costs fortunes and presents risks. Everything that doesn't work fluidly, every redundancy, every archaic element, casts a little shadow, he said, and thereby creates a possibility for manipulation. And there is only so much you can protect against physical contact. A thumb drive does not have to be in your computer long, not long at all, to have been in your computer, and change everything. Such is the state of the art.

As she had turned the pages of your ancient sagas Hannah saw gold, rooms full of gold. But money has changed, Measurement said, the gold standard is gone, and all that money has now is itself. Your wealth had become modern, the gold changed into air and algorithms long ago. Measurement said that just as money should not be too dirty, it should also not be too clean. There is a golden mean and you were, alas, not far from it. They have the money of politicians in their bank, Measurement said, guaranteed not just by some vague entity, not just by some agency with one jurisdiction or another, but by the motive force of the world, the market itself. To trigger such an avalanche, changing ones into zeroes, requires specialists, specialists of sacking, the Envoy said. You need not only to create instability, you need to freeze the stabilizers. You need Defamation.

What is Defamation? Hannah asked.

A company.

Of what? she asked

Criminals, he said. More or less. You need to change how a huge number of people think so that you can change how a select number of them act. You need the Syrls to be, if only for an hour, politically untouchable. You need people to step away, to sit back and watch, and for this you need a great fire. And for a great fire you need great fuel. The good news is that there is wood in abundance and it is very dry. Like fire prevention, the suppression of scandal is itself a risk, as sooner or later there is lightning, and if the underbrush is dry enough, if the winds are favorable, the fire can be seen from space.

Sometimes we found the grievous thing quickly, some bright bit of pure criminality discovered as Annika and Hannah made the rounds, their pockets full of flash drives, helping Measurement move onto the many systems of the Syrls. People really cannot refrain from recording things that surprise them, and your family did surprising things. We had even more on some of you than you saw, withheld for the sole reason that it strained belief. This was most true of Sixten. The more we came to know him, the more repugnant he became, which is remarkable if you consider that the reason we were hacking his email in the first place was rape. Given access to his personal communications, including ones that he would delete, we had a feast of plenty in the way of damaging information. Sixten had always wished to be truly famous. Hannah would grant his wish.

Measurement found things buried and buried things to be found: the misuse of money, privilege, protection, connection. And Defamation made sure all would know, when the time came, which way to turn in the labyrinth of your misinformation. Defamation needed to seem, at the outset, like chance, and so began slowly, priming the public, awakening suspicions, creating associations, planting stories, planting the seeds of doubt with what they called micro-scandals. There is a natural crescendo to outrage, they said. Better not to sneak up on them, better to prime them. The timing and types of revelations were planned with care. The degree to which the stories would be damaging to you would be the degree to which they would be interesting to others, so they had to be sure to make you not just bad, but entertaining. *Schadenfreude*, as the Wise One said, is universal, even if only the Germans had the bad taste to name it. Those whose day was full of frustration for buses missed and traffic and waste and confusion and humiliation and boredom and delusion and insult and all the forms of class violence, those who wanted an answer to why the world was so cruel, so confused, were to be given one: you.

Defamation studied flow, studied the currents in the flood of words and images uploaded every moment of every day, flowing constantly. They had been tracking, with care, how a story, such as one about a certain Syrl with a certain substance and a certain nanny, might get an extraordinary amount of retweeting and reposting in no time at all, something, Defamation said, that would be appropriate for an earthquake in rural China, and if that bit of gossip moves enough within the first hours it triggers sensors which relay it down the line and in no time everyone in rural China knows your nanny, even if no one knows why. We will make their scandal phosphorescent, they said. That's our job. We have been preparing it for the Wreckoning, but in the meantime there is a beta version ready for the House of Syrl. With the remaining bitcoin we paid those who control flow to control yours, to see to it that in the swirling spaces of the internet you would be unmistakable. Defamation, they said, has a short but brilliant half-life. Whether they believe it is just a drop of justice in a sea of injustice or that it is the first sign of universal harmony, they will watch, which is all you need.

Had Hannah become a marine biologist or a horse trainer or a cabinet minister or a first responder I think she would have excelled, but not so greatly as she did at industrial espionage, not so greatly as she did at war. Far from laming her genius, the bright blood of anger sharpened it. The sheer creativity of her malice was shocking to all who saw it, and all who saw it wanted to see more. People speak of being confident as though it were a good in itself, as though being confident in capacities you didn't possess or outcomes you could not produce would get you anywhere but into trouble. But being confident that you will win when you are better is something else entirely. It is accessible to reason. And it is moving. Sitting in front of the screen, tapping a pencil, twirling it with her fingers, Hannah would whisper, *I'm going to ruin you.* She would sit for hour upon hour, moving through your systems, scouting, tracking, hunting you. And when her body would grow stiff and her vision blurry from scanning your screens she would stand up and stretch and then sink down on her haunches, strong like the Ottawa, and she would look in Sedna's golden eyes and, calmed by the contact, she would go back to the work of war.

You ask whether anyone tried to stop her. I did. Once. I wanted to kill Sixten and be done with it. I mentioned mission drag. She said mission drag was when you do not know your objective. When you know your objective it is called the long game. I said that you don't march across seven Roman provinces, three large rivers, two dangerous mountain ranges with an army of Africans to tell them, once you've arrived in the green hills of Italy, once you have arrived where none have ever been, 'you know, I'm not really feeling it, let's go back to Spain.' Many are waiting on you, I told her. But that is not necessity. We were on the beach, the sun setting serene, getting ready to take the boards and the dog and walk up to the house, light a fire, eat and drink and touch and sleep, and I asked her, with the goldening light on her freckles, her eyes calm, merry, mischievous, full of the ocean, whether it wouldn't be better to let it go. We could stay right there. We could walk away from it without even moving. She was quiet a long time, watching the sky and the water, then she told me in Potawatomi that she understood, but she had to move her canoe.

You may remember seeing Hannah in the hospital as your brother was dying. She remembered you. She thanked the Wise One and thanked him again and he said it is the most natural thing in the world, everyone learns from someone else, it's the whole idea, there was no need to thank him. And when he saw she couldn't stop crying he asked her why she was so angry. Because I want you to do it for me, she said, to stay for me, to live in pain for me. I want you to will it, she said, I want you to want it so much it happens. To see me finish. Because I'm close, she said. I've been hunting all night and I'm so close to my kill. And he opened his wise eyes wide and said, child, how could you ever imagine I wouldn't stay if I could? You have been my favorite thing in this world. But it does not work like that. Not at all. I can feel it everywhere in me, the leaving. I'm late. And with her nose running and her eyes streaming she walked all those flights to the roof of the hospital and fell on her knees and screamed until her voice was gone, pounded until her hands bled. And when she looked up, her knuckles bleeding, the blood mixed with tears on her face, she said now there's no more Wise One, now it was time for war.

There were Portents. Huge flocks of starlings arrived, converged, descended, departed. One night an alarm went off in the street below. The machines are already reacting, Hannah said. The time is nigh. And then one morning it was there, resplendent, the shape of our occasion. People in Rome knew that war was upon them when they awoke to find the great statue of Jove changed, his face painted bright red like blood. Within hours Justin was mobilized, Annika weaponized, time to launch all the ships, light the fuses, detonate the charges, awaken the sleepers, begin the party. You had wheeled us in, the sun had set, it was time to come out and burn Troy.

The movement of your money required moving the rest, required personal and political and sexual and ecological scandals entering into sympathetic vibration. Dying gorillas, dying people, sale of arms, contempt for life, rainforests clear-cut, coral reefs bleached, waters fouled, your name in every mouth, every newspaper, every site, tweet, post, with all those terrible images, the whole world hanging on your words. Once the margin call was announced Hannah had Measurement release the rest, like firebombs, lighting up your night, terabytes of texts, images, emails, an irresistibly graphic twitter trail of photos, tweets, screenshots of snapchats, clips, police reports, footage all moving faster and faster thanks to the winds of Defamation swirling them about until the circulation of the stories itself became a news item, ensuring it was front and center as your politician walked to the podium.

To be sure, however, for she needed to be sure, Hannah went back to where she came from, to the center, to Ecuador. It was virtually impossible to reach, and after all those hours in all those types of transport, big plane and small and daredevil bus and burro and boat and canoe we were somewhere far beyond exhausted. We waited, sweating, attracting attention, until Consuela saw the moment in the proceedings when Hannah might speak. She asked Hannah with her eyes if she was ready, and Hannah paled, and nodded, and Consuela walked across the old parquet of that hall, paint chipped, stucco fallen, eaten away by the moisture of all that Amazon and she gave Hannah the microphone. She said, tell them what you want, daughter, holding the microphone just near enough so that all present heard her say *hija,* so that the respect they had for her be extended to the woman she had held as a child and raised as her own. When Hannah began to speak even the children fell silent. A great many people passed through their lands who spoke one Spanish or another, but none had ever arrived who spoke their Spanish, with its rhythm and accents and life all its own. The elders remembered the freckled child, remembered her father at her age, and to them it seemed cyclical and thus propitious. Hannah's father had asked them to trust him, to act with him, and they had not. And as soon as he was gone they saw how right he had been, how quickly everything changed, how quickly the Syrls sucked the life out of their ground, leaving them with nothing for it but ruin. And now they were to be given a second chance, the world sending them a Syrl with an even sharper mind and an even more radical idea than her father's. Which, as you can see, they liked.

What does wealth like yours cost the world? Why is it so warm, so cold, so wet, so dry? Why are the animals dying? *Who caused the harm?* is no longer a question anyone can answer, given the harm, and how interwoven it is with all the weight of the world. For harm is ultimately just what everyone wants. But no one wants to hear that, Hannah said. They want to know *who, when, why*. And that, she said, is what we will give them. You call it a scapegoat. We call it a start.

Some news outlets accepted our anonymous gifts, bright bows wrapped round them, stories that could write themselves. Most needed to find things on their own, so we seeded their grounds and set the timer for a general strike in the Amazon. No political power could come to your aid with scandals of that sort, and so none did. She knew that your ties would snap like a sail pulled loose in a gale, flapping madly, like a boom swinging from side to side, leaving you dead in the water for our visit to the bank. Her prediction was that at least seven and perhaps all fourteen members would sell stock, not wanting to go down with the dragon ship, at which point she would detonate her final charge and then, she said, it will calve like a glacier.

Sixten's suicide was always a special part of the plan. As you may have guessed, your son did not die by his own hand. He died by mine. And Justin's. We had waited, for Hannah needed him to live so that she could use his instability, his greed, his ability to influence others. It had been her first rule. No killing of Sixten before the endgame. When we arrived he was defiant. Do what you want, he said. I like pain, he said. Justin said that was like saying because you like swimming you like drowning. Sixten grew expansive. He said that it was the most intense pleasure of his life, that he would kill us both, that we'd die in great pain, that he was sorry, that he hated himself for it, that she had fought him, that he would do it again, that he would give each of us a million kroner. Justin had a gift for violence. It might not be a good gift, but that does not make it any less a gift. And your son saw this gift. He could see nothing in Justin's eyes that looked like anything but pain, so he looked to mine. Justin was not there to talk. Whereas I had business to conclude.

Your son asked shrewd things and so I presented him with his options. So that you not get your hopes up, you die either way, I told him. It is a matter of how you want to spend your last moments on earth. In prolonged and terrific pain? It is frightening, after all, to have things put in your body. Or facing the blade, a breath and then gone before you even have time to hear the sound. You pick. After which he became quite cooperative, dutifully conveying to us the passwords and the locations of every item we were seeking. He logged in, made the trades, confirmed them with his call, sent a final email and then, as the coroner wrote, Sixten Syrl took his own life.

The Wise One said that vengeance is very diverse and so the Greeks had different gods and goddesses for it. Those who punished violence to one's own blood were the most terrible. They had the faces of children and the Greeks called them the Gentle Ones because it was too scary to say their real name, which was the Furies. How it must have slipped like fear through your veins when you saw the Furies, when you saw what there was to see, you, matriarch, architect of the alliance. And with all the world thinking you were bending under the weight of misfortune and circumstance, you were bending under the furious weight of her. Even you must concede that her last move was brilliant, made as it was by anticipating your reaction. She risked all she had accomplished, all she had aligned on her prediction of your decision, created all that turbulence, smoke, static, instability, chaos, and outrage, counting on your doing just as you did. The Romans would have won the battle of Cannae easily had they held the line. But they didn't.

How the forgotten must now surround you, everywhere and always, what you see a scintillatingly bright line in the night of all you have known and thought and felt, all those years, too much to recall other than under exceptional circumstances, such as these. Some hold that the deepest human obligation to Creation is to repair the damage men do by being men. Hannah liked to think of it in these terms. It is far from the peaceful resignation advocated by the major world religions. Vengeance is a selfish and childish pleasure whose force stems from the greatest sin, that of pride. You can see it that way. But she didn't. Neither do I.

The Wise One told us that after Alexander conquered all, conquered Greece and Egypt and the empire of the Persians, the Tigris, the Euphrates, all the lands beyond the crescent and on the farthest shores of India, staring out to sea he fell down and wept in the sand because there was nowhere left to conquer. Hannah, for her part, was delighted. She did not have some dark venom gliding through her veins, was not born lacking some natural connection to the notions of family and love. On the contrary. For were she simply indifferent to such things her vengeance would hardly have taken the form it did. When shown just how terrible the world might be—and I trust you will agree being raped by your uncle must count among the terrible things the world has to offer—it was not the world she turned against, but you. And you, with all your sight, didn't see it. You did not see what you had done to her, and thus what she would do to you. Perhaps it seemed impossible to give him up, your first-born, your worst. Fierce love of one's own surpasses all reason, as the Wise One said. You must have told yourself that they were just confused words from a frightened girl in a vicious world she was too young to understand. They must sound different now.

The Wise One told us that Caesar and Hannibal lived two centuries apart, were active in the same areas and while alive were of equally universal fame. Of Caesar we know a huge amount. We know of his youth and his family and his Rubicon and how he fought his way around the Mediterranean, we know about him in Britain, in Gaul, in Germania, in Italy and Greece and Egypt, we know about how much his friends loved him and that some of them killed him and about Cleopatra. We know about him seeing six thousand slaves crucified on the road from Capua to Rome so that there be no more Spartacus. We know his eyes were dark like those of a bird of prey, we know when he began balding, his dining habits, dozens of his lovers, his wives, his banking details.

We even have a book he wrote himself about France and all the people he killed there. But of Hannibal we know virtually nothing. Two historians accompanied him on his campaigns, one Greek and one Carthaginian, and they wrote of what they saw, wrote of something so impressive, so alarming, so purely hostile and disparaging to Rome that after Hannibal's death the Romans burned every trace of their writings with such fury that today we know nothing of them except through distant glimmers in the inspired Latin of the Romans who read them. This means that the world does not know what Hannibal was like other than by his acts, which were of breathtaking scale, success and violence. Like Hannah's.

The end should be interesting. Think of all the famous names now gone. Names from books, names of lines, Bourbons, Byrons, Gracchi, all gone. You will have a few hangers-on who will be, I expect, more of an embarrassment than a consolation. A penumbra of awe surrounds even the smallest Syrl, as Hannah said, and that's supposed to be good for them? Many will do surprising things. Most will languish. The world will like it. It is said that the antlers of Irish elk grew so heavy that they could no longer lift their heads, now extinct.

We had a wake for your brother. Annika said that the Wise One would have wanted a question and so Hannah asked all present how they would die if they could choose. Which means I know how Hannah wanted to die. Annika went first. She thought for a moment, and I was guessing opiate overdose but she said she'd like best to fly a fighter jet into the side of a mountain, a big one, in the Himalayas. She thought Annapurna sounded nicest. Justin said he would like to die ninety seconds after having kicked a goal in Rio's Maracana stadium and as he looked up at all those people he had just made so happy, their hearts warm, his would stop. Hannah went last. I don't care how, she said. But I hope it is like a bear, she said. I hope it is sudden, whenever it is, even if I am as old as the Old One I do not want a slow death. I hope it is like a great big bear, fast, strong, smiling with his beautiful head, breath rippling the air, the animal smell of him, the ground shaking from him. That is what she wanted in death, and that is what she got.

The lives of warriors end in blood. How did Caesar die? How did Hannibal? War breeds war, hate hate, vengeance vengeance, violence violence. Everyone knows that, she said. When we were little we would take sheets of your daughter-in-law's architecture paper, spread it on her desk and draw the world. We would map the seas and the skies, trace the movement of the stars, the fur trade, the Ottawa, the trails of the Old One. I remember one day the sun, golden, orange, amber, fire, streaming through the windows. I had always liked it there. It was peaceful, the space clear and organized and reflective, and there were windows looking out into the woods and down at the creek. It smelled nice, being the source of the house's subtle aromatherapy. We were drawing there and Hannah handed me a letter she had written on one of those huge sheets. It had an Indian brave of winter followed by one of spring, magical geese, the island of the turtle. I would be, she wrote, her husband and we would have nineteen puppies, and she named them.

Hannah almost drowned once, in Brazil, off an island south of Rio, many hours out to sea. We took a boat there because the surf was famous and all the Brazilians told us not to go. It had been cursed for all memory, haunted by spirits from the first days, made a leper colony, then a prison, then an insane asylum, and was then more or less deserted. No roads, no cars, dense jungle, many animals, minimal accommodation, one sailboat a day. The first morning we rose with the birds and crossed the island on a very faint path. There were snakes that looked like vines. There were other snakes that looked like snakes, and scorpions and army ants and tree trunks weaponized with spines and giant fruit bats which weren't dangerous but still and the canopy was alive with birds and monkeys all different, capuchin, howler, spider monkeys, all following our motions. It had been far more difficult than we expected and had taken hours. When we arrived at the famous beach on the other side of the island we were proud and fell asleep on the sand. When I woke up Hannah was gone. While I was waiting for her to return, unconcernedly scanning the handful of others strung along the long arcing beach, surprised there were no surfers, Hannah was dying. She had begun to swim, drowsily, and been pulled by a current, a conveyor belt of water, there being reasons why the Brazilians thought the island cursed, and it pulled her far out. She had to let it take her scarily far, towards open ocean, towards Africa. This is how it happens, she said she said. And then the water let her loose, the current changed, and she was free. And far. She bobbed a moment, she said, seeing it, taking in how much water there was between her and the beach, between her and the island, seeing how she would have to swim to stay out of the current, and as the fear of it arrived so too did the fury, she said, and she took a deep breath, stretched her body long and swam. The water is my home, she said she said. I live here, she said she said. And she swam, all that water under her, all those hours, watching the sun get lower she made her body like a thing of the sea, and with the sun dangerously low, angry, she arrived at what had sent her out there, the mountainous surf, huge swells that made her sick to see, the surf that made the beach famous. When I found her she was laying face down on the beach, hugging it. She lifted her head and her expression was blank in a way I had never seen. Once a day a sailboat stopped at a nearby cove, our only way back if we did not want to walk through the jungle in the dark. I asked her if she was ok. She said, I almost died. I said if we want the boat we have to run. We ran. It took an hour to sail back to the far side of the island, and Hannah held the rigging, watching the island as we hugged its coast, watching the birds and the monkeys in the trees, watching the sea, serene, smiling, her freckles bright, and she told me what it was for her to live.

The longest period of time I ever went without seeing Hannah was 94 days, now surpassed. The end of the separation was at a wedding, a far-away one. I went right from the airport to the station and took a train going north, following the river, broad, stately, rural, green. I was in no mood. On the plane I had watched The Wedding Singer, in Italian, and wept. I listened to the randomness of the music on my phone and remembered going to a concert with

Hannah in the middle of ruined Detroit, with high levels of decrepitude and danger and seeing Jimmy under a table, watching the concert from the balcony, through its chipped columns, glorying in it, and how we sat behind him, protecting him, enjoying the show.

The ceremony took place beside an old barn. I liked the silence of Jewish marriage, I liked the circles, the breaking glass. I was given a cocktail with elderflower and I wandered over to a paddock and a horse stopped grazing and came over and gently lifted my tie in its mouth and there was Hannah. I always exhaled a little when I saw her, excited that it could begin, whatever it was. When we were little I asked her why she had been surprised when she first saw me and she said because I was her friend.

She pointed to where to meet her and the barn was falling down and the blue was deepening and it smelled of hay and horses and summer and she slipped out of her dress and the cicadas were loud and it was as in the beginning. For as long as I can remember Hannah's voice was the most soothing sound in the world and when there would be a terrible thing she was always there, fast, so fast I didn't know how, and she would look me so hard in the eyes that I had to look back, and only then would her body relax, showing me it was fine, you are safe, warm, like a wolf.

I remember only vaguely, like a thin band of bright light at the horizon, the world without her, which is to say the one before her. I remember running on the beach in the night to Lake Superior, the mother of all fresh water. I remember diving into it, flopping like a seal in the night, and my mother's arms slippery and warm, and that is the start. I have other memories of a time before Hannah, of a cow with its eye glossy and dark, of sunlight, of the smell of my father, but my real beginning is with her. I miss my sister and how humid the nights were and the house from which the world grew. I miss the Old One, the Wise One, her. I'm late. I wish you a long life.

My last wish is that you share it. For if you make known that you were ruined not by random misfortune but instead by your exceptionally gifted grand-daughter, then her name will live on as the architect of your fall, as the definitive end of your line. Then children can hear of how she rode right down to where no Northerner had ever stood before and lit the whole vast, organized, powerful and above all dangerous thing that was your family on fire. And then she whispered *return*.

ABOUT THE AUTHOR

Leland de la Durantaye lives in Los Angeles. This is his debut novel.